HEAR NO EVIL

HEAR NO EVIL

Playing With Fire

Kate Chester

SCHOLASTIC INC.
New York Toronto London Auckland Sydney

No part of this publication may be reproduced in whole or in part, or stored in a retrieval system, or transmitted in any form or by any means, electronic, mechanical, photocopying, recording, or otherwise, without written permission of the publisher. For information regarding permission, write to Scholastic Inc., 555 Broadway, New York, NY 10012.

ISBN 0-590-87992-8

12 11 10 9 8 7 6 5 4 3 2 1   7 8 9/9 0 1 2/0

Printed in the U.S.A.   01

First Scholastic printing, April 1997

To The Reader:

Sara Howell is profoundly, postlingually deaf (meaning she lost her hearing after she learned to speak). She is fluent in American Sign Language (ASL), and English. She can read lips.

When a character speaks, quotation marks are used: "Watch out for that bus!" When a character signs, *italics* are used to indicate ASL: *Watch out for that bus!* Quotation marks and *italics* indicate the character is signing and speaking simultaneously: *"Watch out for that bus!"*

Unless the sign is described (for example: Sara circled her heart. *I'm sorry . . .*), the italicized words are translations of ASL into English, not literal descriptions of the grammatical structure of American Sign Language.

HEAR NO EVIL

Playing With Fire

Chapter 1

The surgical gloves fit like a second skin. Pulling the kitchen match from its box, he sucked in a breath. The snake was back in his brain, a coil of anger, ready to strike. It made it hard to think. When the snake came back there was only one thing to do.

He scanned his flashlight one last time over the machinery in the garage of the Radley City Parks Department. The mowers, the trucks, even the snowblowers had tanks filled with gasoline.

Just like the last time, and the time before that, he struck two matches and blew them out. He stared at the tiny blaze from the third match, then threw it onto the gasoline-soaked rags. He held his breath, and with a sharp, familiar hiss the snake leaped from his brain to the rags. Orange and yellow flames sped over the rags and up the wall.

He grabbed his can of extra rags, snapped off the flashlight, and ran outside and across the deserted park. By the time he was at a safe distance, the garage was engulfed. An explosion even he couldn't have imagined sent towers of flames into the sky. With a roar, windows blew out. Burning timbers tumbled out over the picnic area of Radley's Dexter Sanctuary.

He couldn't wait for the morning news to see what they said about him this time. He'd make the headlines again in the *Gazette*. The fire marshall would have a statement about him. The arson squad would sift the debris trying to find similarities to the other fires. Attention would finally be paid.

Chapter 2

STORAGE GARAGE BLAZE AT
DEXTER SANCTUARY
DESPITE SERIOUS DEVASTATION FIRE MARSHALL
FINDS LINKS TO EARLIER FIRES

Sara Howell reread the headlines as she waited for the traffic light to change. The *Radley Gazette* was propped for display in the newspaper box on the street corner. Three weeks since the fire and it was still making headlines. Sara shivered, wondering who would do such a thing.

The minute the light changed, she urged her golden retriever Tuck forward and crossed the intersection toward home. It was getting late — too late to be out walking

Tuck. This was no time to contemplate where the arsonist might strike again.

She hadn't meant to walk so far, but the spring night was warm; she'd been lost in thoughts of weekend plans. She rowed for the Radley Academy crew team and Bret Sanderson had suggested a river picnic in his powerboat after her practice on Saturday.

Thoughts of an afternoon with Bret disappeared, however, as she noticed pedestrian traffic had thinned to nothing. She made a mental note not to walk this way again unless it was high noon. But then, independence would come only when she was comfortable on these streets, in her own neighborhood, even when the sun went down. It just took practice. She stopped long enough to refasten the barrette that held her shoulder-length brown hair.

Rowing kept her in great shape and walking Tuck before she went to bed helped to kill her pent-up energy. Tonight they'd gone farther than usual and taken a new route. She just hadn't realized how deserted it would be.

There was nothing waiting at home except the review sheet for her biology test in the morning. Her brother Steve had planned to go to his fitness center after working late at the police station. He had to cover for the arson squad detectives who had been called back by the fire marshall. He wouldn't tell her much, but she knew Ed Wilkins, the fire marshall, had been working night and day to tie the Dexter Sanctuary fire to the others. Another shiver slid down her back and she looked over her shoulder.

A fire in a document room of the Radley Library made the news because smoke and water had ruined much of the historic collections the blaze hadn't reached. The room was located in the area of the building where Sara had met Bret, who had worked there part-time. He attended Penham School and took a break from the library to lead their basketball team. After the fire, his parents put a stop to his job at the library.

The Blue Onion went up in flames at four in the afternoon two weeks later. The popular restaurant had been packed with Radley University and area high school students including two of Sara's closest friends, Keesha Fletcher and Liz Martinson. No one had been killed, but there had been a few injuries. Sara knew from the newspaper accounts that two extinguished matches had been found near the wastebasket where the blaze began. Both fires — the one in the library and the one at the Blue Onion — had been started with gasoline-soaked rags. She shook her head and tried to think of something else, but it was difficult. Somewhere in the city was someone who thrived on setting off that kind of destruction.

She tried once again to shift her thoughts to Bret. She'd been dating the handsome athlete since her permanent return to Radley last September. She could have used him beside her right now. At first Steve had insisted that Tuck's last walk of the night was his responsibility, or the doorman's. John O'Connor had often filled in for her brother or her father during the years she was away at boarding school. But those years were gone.

She and Steve had lost their mother years earlier and Detective Paul Howell had been killed at the end of the summer. Overnight, Sara's twenty-two-year-old brother, who had already followed their father to the detective bureau of the Radley Police Department, became her guardian and surrogate parent. Almost a full school year had passed and they were still adjusting.

She and Tuck crossed another street and started along the last commercial block. The wind picked up. Chocolate. The night shift of Buckeye Foods bakery must be in full swing. The bakery was blocks away, but when the wind was right, the delicious smell of baking cookies traveled for miles.

Sara stopped under a streetlight to check her watch. She and Tuck had been gone for forty-five minutes. If Steve had called and she wasn't home, he'd be worried. If he'd already made it home from the gym, he'd be pacing in the living room or looking out the front windows watching the street.

She shortened the leash and quickened her step, always alert. This block was even more deserted then the last one. A single bus passed; there wasn't a pedestrian in sight. Definitely time to head for home. Tuck stopped. He thrust his nose in the air. Chocolate, you silly dog, Sara thought. She inhaled and nudged him forward. He balked. Something was spooking Tuck.

Chills started across her shoulder blades; her heart raced. She looked up at the pattern of dark windows and shuddered. It was as if a thousand eyes stared down at her. Tuck was trained to alert her to more important things than the aroma from bakery ovens half a mile away. While she tried to figure out what it was, she pulled him with her into a doorway.

Sara waited. She took deep breaths and counted to ten, scanning — always scanning — from left to right. Nothing. No one. Any detective's daughter knew better than to huddle in the shadows. She should be standing at the curb, under the streetlights, but the solid feel of the wall behind her settled her pulse. She let out a long, ragged breath and tugged the leash. Tuck wouldn't budge. Sara glanced along the closed storefronts, fighting the urge to bolt and drag him with her. For the first time in weeks an image of boarding school flashed in her brain: her safe, snug room, her roommate. Her heart began to pound again. There was no more boarding school cocoon. In the six years since her mother's death, the Edgewood School for the Deaf had kept her safe and taught her well, but now Steve was all she had. The confines of the school halfway across the country were no longer enough. She needed Edgewood, but she needed Steve more. She calmed herself with shallow, even breaths. She might be on an unfamiliar, dark, deserted street, but this was Radley; this was home.

She rubbed her hand on her jeans. She had her brother; she had Bret. Her closest friend through everything was Keesha, and the whole Fletcher family lived right across the hall at Thurston Court, the apartment building she and Steve lived in. And I'd love to have any one of you right here, Sara thought as she yanked Tuck out of the doorway and back under the streetlight.

The retriever nudged her thigh with his nose. He'd nudged her a hundred times at home to tell her the doorbell had sounded, the phone had rung, even that she'd left the bathwater running. Now she tried to urge him forward. Suddenly he reared up on his haunches and landed one paw on her arm, the other on her leg. She staggered back against a parking meter, as much from shock and fear as Tuck's weight.

In the ten years since she'd lost her hearing to meningitis, her visual perception had sharpened. She stared, studied. She clenched her jaw. Tuck raised his head, pointing his muzzle high. Under the lamplight she watched the tip of his nose quiver. Smell, not sound. Tuck smelled something that put her in danger.

The wind shifted and took the chocolate aroma with it. The hair on her neck tingled. Tuck's sense of smell, so much more powerful than a human's, had picked up what she just now sensed. Under the chocolate was the unmistakable smell of charred timber.

Chapter 3

Sara tightened Tuck's leash, tempted to kneel and throw her arms around his neck in gratitude. With her heart still racing she took another breath. She smelled charred wood, and ash, but no smoke. She hurried along the block. Stores passed in her peripheral vision as she kept her eyes on Tuck. As they reached the corner the smell grew sharp, unmistakable.

Sara brought the tips of her fingers into the palm of her hand, then snapped her fingers. *Good dog,* she signed to him. *Good dog.* She ruffled his fur to let him know she understood his warning. EAST END GALLERY still flapped in gold lettering from a ripped awning over the boarded-up entrance. Covering the display window, which normally held the works of prominent area artists, there were sheets of plywood, hand-lettered with the words CLOSED DUE TO FIRE.

Tuck nudged her once again. She patted him. No danger, Tuck. Her heart slowed to its normal rate. Even in the dark she could see that the Dumpster to the side of the gallery was overflowing with jagged pieces of beams, planks, and scrap lumber. Then she remembered. The East End Gallery had been gutted a few days after the blaze at the sanctuary. The smell in the air was fresh due to demolition, not embers.

Sara made it back to Thurston Court relieved and fascinated. As they rode the elevator, she unsnapped Tuck's leash and shook out her arms as if she could shake the tension that had kept her on edge for the last twenty minutes. When they stopped at the seventh floor, the elevator door slid open and Tuck automatically started down the hall for their apartment.

Sara stopped as she spotted Keesha. Her

best friend was lugging a canvas bag of recyclable bottles in the direction of the incinerator room. She waved and nodded toward Sara's apartment.

Sara signed *S, BROTHER?*, their name sign for Steve. She raised her eyebrows to make it a question.

Keesha nodded. *He came over to see if I had gone with you to walk Tuck.*

Keesha was the only one of Sara's friends who had no trouble understanding her muffled speech. She was also nearly fluent in American Sign Language, which she'd studied and practiced with Sara over the years. The two of them compromised by combining both languages.

Sara looked at the Howell front door. *I was hoping I'd get home before Steve. Beautiful night. I came past the block with the art gallery fire. Tuck scared me to death. Fire! Fire! he thought. He kept trying to warn me.*

"East End Gallery?" Keesha said slowly. Sara nodded.

Keesha frowned. *Dad's construction com-*

pany has been scheduled to repair the damage for weeks. All the stores in that block have been shut down because of structural damage. "When the fire marshall started finding similarities in the other city fires, the insurance company for the gallery held up payment until there was another full investigation to prove it wasn't burnt down for insurance money." *Messed up Dad's construction schedule.*

Was it arson?

Keesha shook her head. "No. Bad wires. Electrical. Not related." She tapped her forehead and raised her index finger. *Understand?*

Sara nodded and congratulated her on her ASL as the Howell apartment door opened. As Keesha said good night and continued down the hall with her bottles, Steve Howell ushered Tuck inside and waited for his sister. His attempt to look casual and unconcerned might have worked except for his eyes. His clear blue gaze was focused directly on Sara.

"Nice night. I walked Tuck farther than usual," she said. *Nice night*, she added with her hands. For extra measure she circled her heart, the sign for *sorry,* and then pantomimed lifting weights. "I thought you'd still be at the gym. Good workout?"

"No. Lousy as a matter of fact. I came home early."

"I hope you didn't worry." But Steve's handsome face told her otherwise.

"I worry even when I'm not home, Sara." *Too late. Too dark,* he signed for emphasis. "You should have taken Keesha with you."

Keesha had homework, Sara replied. She touched his arm. "I can't always be with somebody, Steve. I'm sixteen. I'm doing fine." She poked him playfully. "You're the one who isn't."

"I'm the one with all the responsibility!"

She read his lips. "Tonight I walked the block where the gallery fire was." With a dull ache Sara glanced at the photograph of her father on the corner table. "These fires make the kind of case Dad would have loved. His kind of detective work."

Sara brought it up to see if she could get Steve to talk. She missed her father, and she missed the long rambling letters he had sent weekly to Edgewood, letters that described cases, clues, instinct . . . all the things that had made her want to study criminology herself.

She frowned at the fatigue in her brother's face. Steve never wanted to discuss the details of any case, as if details from police work might rub off and put her in jeopardy.

She followed him into the den. "Keesha said her father's been waiting to get started on the gallery."

Steve frowned.

"Gallery. Artwork."

He nodded that he finally understood. "The fire marshall — Ed Wilkins — has reopened the files on every blaze in the last six months to see if any more can be linked to one arsonist. While it was under investigation, the insurance company put everything on hold. There was smoke and water damage to the whole block. A lot of angry store owners." He scrunched his fingers in front of his face. *Angry.*

She smiled at his ASL. "Any new clues from the storage garage fire at the sanctuary?"

"Nothing new."

She sighed. Even if the arson squad had found a trail that led right to the perpetrator, he wouldn't tell her.

Steve glanced at the clock. *Late. Get to bed. I'll walk Tuck in the morning.*

She touched her lips with her fingertips and dropped her hand forward. *Thank you.* "I know they found traces of the rags at the garage, just like the Blue Onion and the library. How about the kitchen matches?"

Steve shrugged as if he hadn't understood her.

Matches. How many this time?

I understand. It's just not . . . He sighed. *Late. Get to bed,* he repeated.

Sara snapped off the light and went into the hall with him. "Steve, I'm interested. Dad would have talked about it."

He scowled. "Dad would have written to you about it. You were halfway across the country then. Big difference."

"This crazy person is only burning buildings." *Angry. Nothing to do with me.*

Nothing? Your boyfriend worked at the li-

brary. Two of your best friends were at the Blue Onion. Could have been you at either place. I'm the cop, not you, Sara. One of the most important things I've learned is that you can't ever think it can't be you.

Chapter 4

The next morning Sara was late. Keesha's mother was head of the Radley Academy Lower School, but rather than ride in with the Fletchers, Sara had chosen to review her biology as she walked to school. The delay had come from trying to weave her hair into a French braid. Steve's feeble attempt to help had put them both in hysterics. It felt good to laugh, but it felt even better to leave her brother relaxed and in a good mood. He hadn't even signed *Be careful* as she'd left the apartment.

The minute she hit the spring wind outside Thurston Court, she wondered why she'd bothered with such an intricate hairstyle.

Sections of braid worked loose as she crossed the first intersection. Radley Academy's dress code allowed a choice of a green kilt or khaki pants and she was glad she'd chosen pants and added her crew jacket against the cool morning air.

The solitary walk gave Sara the time she needed to concentrate on her biology. Commuters waited for their buses as the streets clogged with cars in the morning rush hour. She took the direct route to campus and chided herself over last night's fear. She was sure seeing the gallery in the daylight would make her laugh at the chills and Tuck's frantic nudging.

Halfway to school she checked her watch and decided to cut through the alley behind the houses on Reynolds Street. It would shave half a block from her trip.

The familiar shortcut was lined with garages and fences that gave the small backyards privacy. Trash cans sat in twos and threes. Occasionally there was enough gap in a fence so that she could glimpse into the hidden gardens. A single car pulled out and headed for the intersection, reminding her that she had to hurry.

The wind whipped dirt into tiny tornados and scattered unraked leaves. Suddenly, Sara smelled smoke. Unlike the night before, it wasn't damp cinders and ash. It was fresh, sharp and close. She turned. As the breeze died, a thin line of smoke drifted in the air from the yard of the second house. A six-foot board fence blocked her view, but she could smell barbecue sauce. It was an odd time to have a grill going, she thought, but maybe somebody liked steak and eggs for breakfast. She grinned as she hurried along. Barbecue for breakfast was none of her business.

She checked her watch again; there was no time to lose. Mrs. Andrews, the interpreter who accompanied her to class, would already be waiting. Sara shifted her backpack and hurried through the alley to the busy avenue at the end. She tapped her foot impatiently as she waited for the traffic to clear so she could cross. A school bus rumbled past, then a delivery truck, and a stream of commuters. She could still smell the smoke. She imagined her brother's flying fingers. *None of your business,* he would sign. *Your business is getting to school on time. Your business is meeting your interpreter and getting a decent grade on your biology test.*

Steve was right, but it didn't keep her from turning around while she waited. This time instead of the single strand, the smoke had thickened to a haze. Clouds of it had wrapped the back porch. The wind flattened a blanket of smoke against the house's wooden siding. Sara shoved hair from her eyes in alarm. She could see tips of flames at the top of the fence. She tried to think. Barbecue or no barbecue, the grill was out of control. Flames that high threatened the whole porch, not to mention the room above it, all of it made of wood.

She turned around and waved frantically at the traffic, hoping someone would stop. Two children in a minivan waved back.

No. Fire! she signed to the oblivious drivers. Did they think she was flagging down a bus? Waiting for a car pool? She gave up on the cars and yanked her backpack off her shoulders. Even if she could get a car to stop, there was the constant problem of making herself understood. There wasn't time to deal with the befuddled expressions of strangers as they tried to decipher her words.

Sara turned back to the alley. Surely someone else had seen the fire. Someone had called the fire department. Maybe sirens were already blasting as fire trucks raced through the morning traffic. She shook her head. The closest firehouse was next to her brother's police station. There'd be no racing in this traffic. The trucks would have to inch their way along as they forced cars to pull over.

She left her pack and ran back down the alley, grateful that she hadn't chosen this morning to wear her kilt. She heaved herself over the fence and into the backyard.

Across the lawn, a kettle-style grill sat on the back porch next to the railing. Flames shot from it and had already started to climb the columns that supported the room above. The sight sent her heart to her throat.

The fire was not just shooting from the grill. The floor of the porch was blackened and a solid wall of flame burned the ceiling. As she pressed her fist against her thundering heart, flames worked their way up the back wall of the house, quickly reaching the second floor. In the corner of a window was the familiar oval "Tot Finder" sticker from the fire department. Flames had reached some child's bedroom.

Thank goodness it's a school day, Sara thought. As she ran toward the porch, she tripped over a paint can laying in the grass. She swore and limped closer, but heat and smoke drove her back. The speed of the fire shocked her into action. She choked and coughed as she wiped tears already streaking her face. In the time it had taken to climb the fence, the back porch had become a solid wall of flames.

She stared at the burglar alarm sticker on the glass-paned back door. Thankfully there was no sign that anyone was inside, but whoever lived there would lose the entire house if the flames continued up the back wall. Adults off to work, kids off to school . . . an empty house would be left with the alarm set. She turned back for the paint can she had just tripped over.

By setting off the alarm, help would come automatically. It was the quickest solution. The smoke swirled again and caught her full in the face. She picked up the can and heaved it as hard as she could at the closest window. Glass shattered. Smoke rushed through the opening.

She took a breath and rubbed her ankle, wondering what to do next. There was traffic out on the streets, but no one would spot these flames from the front until the whole house was blazing. Sara brushed herself off. Heat and smoke drove her into a fit of coughing as she stumbled away from the house. As she took a final look at the flames, the window over the porch opened.

Behind the screen she could just make out the face of a boy. There was a flash of red hair and an elbow as he shielded himself from the blanket of smoke. She saw the palms of his hands flatten as he tried to push out the screen. She saw the look of raw terror and panic as he opened his mouth to scream.

Chapter 5

Sara cupped her hands. "No! Close the window! Front door! Front door!" She pressed her vocal cords with her palm to make sure she'd yelled. She could see the boy call down to her.

Tears, as much from frustration as the smoke, streaked Sara's face. She pounded her ear and looked up at the window. "I'm deaf! Can't hear you! Front door!" she tried again.

The boy blurred behind a fresh cloud of smoke. The window stayed raised, but he turned around and disappeared. Sara coughed and forced herself to wait. A panicked child might run right to her. He'd called out something she couldn't hear. The porch was thick with smoke and framed in fire. She put her hand over her mouth to keep back the choking and tried to hold her breath. Her fear came true. The child opened the back door.

"No!" She screamed. She closed her eyes against the stinging smoke as she took the steps two at a time. Cinders fell on her shoulder from the ceiling as she crossed the porch and pushed him deeper into the house. She slammed the door.

Once inside, she squinted at the terrified redhead. He was still in pajamas and couldn't have been more than ten or eleven. Outside, charred planks of the porch ceiling fell. "Front door," she said. Her throat was raw.

The room was cool, but smoke billowed in through the hole in the window. The unlabeled paint can lay on the floor in a shower of glass. She pushed the boy ahead of her down a hallway toward the front door. No fire. Yet. "Call 911 from next door," she said.

He stared at her.

"I'm deaf. Can you understand me?"

He finally nodded.

"Call 911," she repeated as she flashed the

numbers at him with her fingers. She yanked him by the wrist and rushed out the front door to the closest house.

Moments later they stood together under a maple tree. Although the house next door had been empty, the door had been unlocked and the boy had run right to the phone, obviously familiar with the home. He looked flushed and every bit as terrified as she felt. She first lip-read "my mom," as he spoke, then "my ear hurts."

She felt his feverish forehead and tried to pull him farther away, but he wouldn't budge. By the time Sara looked at the street, cars were stopping.

The boy turned to her. "Sirens. Can you hear the sirens?"

"Fire trucks coming?" she asked slowly.

He nodded and pointed down the street. "I can hear them from over there. My mom will be right back. I'm sick. She went to fill a prescription."

Sara nodded, although she missed part of the conversation again. In any new situation she lost almost fifty to seventy-five percent of lipreading. It didn't matter. His body language and facial expressions told her most of what she needed to know.

Sara took off her jacket and put it around his shoulders. She ran her finger under the emblem of crossed oars. He smiled weakly and pantomimed rowing. She nodded. Anything to keep him occupied. She put her arm around him and tried to ignore the commotion that had begun to break out at the bottom of the sloping lawn behind them.

"I'm Sara," she said slowly.

The boy held her hand. "Charlie. Charlie Gates."

In the next few minutes the fire trucks arrived and parked at the closest hydrant. Sara clutched Charlie as firefighters raced the hoses through the front door and along the side of the house. When the boy suddenly freed himself, Sara turned. A woman with hair as red as Charlie's was racing toward them from a car at the curb. Directly behind her was a white van with WRAD MOBILE NEWS painted on the side. WTCA–ALL NEWS

ALL THE TIME was on another vehicle parked across the street.

Sara sucked in a breath. Blue police lights spun from the top of three squad cars that had just come onto the scene. Then the red sedan of the Radley fire marshall pulled up. The street, lawn, and sidewalk became a blur of scrambling bodies and jacketed firefighters. She was about to turn back to Charlie when her brother's familiar blue Jeep tore around the corner and skidded to a stop.

As Steve got out and ran toward the squad cars, Sara flagged him down. Detective Howell stared at her in amazement.

Sara never made it to school. Steve drove her home to shower, change, and bandage her leg. As soon as she washed away the smoke and grit, he delivered her downtown to the headquarters of the police and fire departments' arson divisions. Her grueling day continued in the interrogation room with the fire marshall and other investigators. Steve even called in Sara's interpreter, Suzanne Andrews, in case Sara couldn't make herself understood. For hours the detectives had her repeat everything she could remember from the moment she'd entered the alley.

When Sara and Steve got back to Thurston Court, they found the phone message light blinking and the tape jammed with requests for interviews. Some savvy reporters even called through the relay operator on Sara's TTY, the telecommunications machine. She took the fire marshall's advice and refused all interviews. Ed Wilkins had explained that in most cases the arsonist fed on the attention his destruction created.

"You shouldn't have done this. You're too generous," Sara said that evening as Emilio Patrone unpacked a box of gourmet sandwiches, drinks, and desserts on the coffee table in the Howells' den and then refused payment.

The owner of the Penn Street Deli, old enough to be her grandfather, brushed off her protests. "Another hero in the family," he said to the group gathered around her. "You make us all proud. Your papa, too, God rest his soul. When I heard, I thought, what can

I do to help? Feed them, of course." He winked.

She hugged the kindly delicatessen owner as Steve tried to get him to stay and watch the newscast with them.

Emilio shook his head. "I can't. I saw it all on the noon broadcast anyway. And Rocco gave me only twenty minutes to make the delivery. Enjoy."

Steve and Sara's relationship with the Patrone brothers went back to their father's earliest days on the police force when Detective Howell had saved Emilio Patrone's life during a burglary. The delicatessen and grocery was half a block from the station and the place Paul Howell, and now his son, most often picked up meals during his erratic work schedule.

By noon, word of the fire had swept through Radley Academy, Penham School, and the rest of the city. Since Sara had spent the day at the police station, Bret, Keesha, Liz Martinson, even Marisa Douglas, the woman who dated Steve, had come over for a firsthand account.

As Emilio left the apartment Bret motioned to the television screen. The face of Charlie Gates flashed into view. *"Look at this, Sara. They're opening with you!"* Bret, who was fluent in ASL because his parents were deaf, signed to Sara as he spoke to the others.

They huddled around the television as the local news continued. Sara grimaced as WRAD ran the tape of her as she took off her crew jacket and put it around Charlie's shoulders. They had caught her pointing out the crossed oars as she tried to keep him calm.

"We told every reporter who called, no interviews," Steve grumbled. "This isn't about Sara. It's about a pyromaniac who's got to be stopped."

Sara shuddered and Steve put his arm around her. Last August the press had hounded both of them when their father died, playing up the fact that since the police lieutenant had been a widower, Steve was now Sara's guardian. Deaf orphan, they'd called her. She still hated the term.

Months later the sports section of the *Gazette* had published a profile on her when she and her teammates won a silver medal at a rowing regatta. This time she was an inspiration. She was tired of the media focusing on her deafness, as if it kept her from leading a normal life.

Sara grimaced as closed captions ran across the bottom of the screen. The television reporter milked every ounce of melodrama she could find.

A deaf teenager taking a shortcut to Radley Academy saved the life of a Reynolds Street child this morning as the Radley arsonist struck again.

The film clip ended and the screen filled with a live remote broadcast from the alley behind Reynolds Street.

This time the fire was set at the home of Radley banker Robert Gates. According to Mrs. Gates, who also works in the financial district, the house is normally empty at that hour. However this morning, eleven-year-old Charlie was home with an ear infection and his mother had just gone to the pharmacy to fill a prescription. Sara Howell, whose brother is a city detective, is also the orphaned daughter of Lieutenant Paul Howell. She was taking a shortcut to Radley Academy along the alley right behind me. Despite the fact that she is profoundly deaf, when Sara smelled smoke she risked her own life. The sixteen-year-old jumped this fence to get into the backyard. Unable to hear whether an alarm was sounding, she broke a window to alert the homeowners . . .

Sara sank to the edge of the couch, unable to eat. Her mouth went dry as the reporter had the camera follow the route she'd taken to get to the house. It didn't seem to bother the reporter at all that Sara and the Gates family had refused to be interviewed.

Despite Sara's heroism, the Gateses had a traumatized child and massive damage to their house. None of them wanted more publicity. Margaret Gates had said what they all knew. An angry, possibly deranged criminal, bold enough to set fires in broad daylight, would be watching the news and reading the paper to see what they'd made of his latest catastrophe.

Chapter 6

Sara's cheeks burned. Her silence hadn't been very effective.

Steve's face was flushed with anger.

You really are a hero, Keesha signed to Sara.

"I was at the right place at the right time, that's all."

The evening news wasn't going to tell her anything she didn't already know. Sara watched the camera scan the back alley a final time. The camera returned to the reporter who looked intently into it. As she spoke, Steve jumped to his feet muttering something at the screen.

As if saving a child weren't enough for Sara Howell, the captions printed out, sources tell us Sara also unlocked a key bit of evidence. She broke the kitchen window with a paint can from the backyard. It was packed with rags soaked in gasoline, a trademark of the arsonist. It's now in the crime lab being studied by the city's forensic specialists. Of course the arson squad is hoping to find fingerprints and other clues to unlock this terrible rash of destruction that has brought Radley to its knees.

Sara tried to chew on her roast beef sandwich as Steve continued to pace. Liz leaned over, wide-eyed. "Did you know what was in the can?"

Sara shook her head. "I tripped on it. When I needed something to break the glass, it was all I could think of. I didn't know what was in it till they told me at the station downtown."

Liz nodded that she'd understood and glanced at Steve, then back to Sara. She scrunched her fingers in front of her face.

Sara nodded. *Yes. He's angry. Really angry.*

Her brother caught their ASL. "You bet

I'm angry. The information about the can is confidential. There's a leak in the arson squad, or else some damn reporter overheard something." He threw up his hands and looked at Sara's friends. "We're dealing with a maniac. Each fire has gotten bigger and more dangerous. That child could have been killed!"

Sara watched her brother. She knew he hadn't said what bothered him the most: She had been the one who thwarted the arsonist's plan.

The group finished their dinner while the news continued. Marisa was due at East End General Hospital; she was an administrative nurse in the Emergency Room. Liz tapped Bret to remind him she was driving him home.

"I'll walk you out to your car," Sara said as she signed to Liz. *"I'm glad you gave me my homework assignments. I need a normal routine back at school."*

"You'll be coming back tomorrow?" Liz asked.

"Yes! Absolutely." She turned to Keesha. *"Both of you would really be a help if you tell everybody I don't want any special treatment and I don't want to talk about the fire. All the details have been on TV. I'm sure it will be in the paper in the morning. That's enough."*

"More than enough," Bret grumbled as they left the apartment for the elevators.

He and Sara exchanged a wary glance. Since she'd started dating him last fall, they'd had more than their share of close calls.

"I assume you want to ride in with Mom, Marcus, and me?" Keesha asked as she crossed the hall to her own front door.

Sara thrust her fist forward. *Yes! See you in the morning. Don't leave without me.*

As they left Keesha and rode down in the elevator, Sara leaned back and watched the floor numbers light up. The fire marshall had told her the Gates family would be moved into a hotel. She wondered how Charlie was doing, having to recover away from the comfort of his own room. Maybe it was just as well. She couldn't imagine that he'd find any comfort there.

Thinking about the kid? Bret signed.

Sara smiled and nodded slowly.

That's just like you. Always thinking about the other guy. Think about yourself, Sara. He looked at her with wide, serious brown eyes before he put his arm around her shoulder.

The hug felt good as she snuggled against Bret. What he really meant was for her to stay away from danger. Sometimes he could be as overly protective as her brother.

The minute Sara crossed the lobby and stepped out into the evening air, a man and woman sprinted toward her from the curb. The woman waved Bret and Liz aside. The man knelt and snapped her photograph. The woman's mouth was moving, but Bret jumped forward and Sara lost the conversation. Steve came up beside her and put his hand out to the photographer. It was then that she realized her brother had called something to Bret.

Sara spun angrily to her brother. *I can handle this myself! I don't need you and Bret to rescue me!* She could tell from Steve's blank expression that he hadn't understood her words. It didn't matter. Her expression had told him enough.

She left the interpreting to Bret and pulled the reporter aside. "I don't have anything to say except that I'm grateful I was able to help stop a tragedy this morning. I'm not a hero; I just happened to be the one in the alley who smelled the smoke. Please just say that I'm glad no one was hurt." She looked directly into the reporter's eyes. "Did you understand all that?"

The reporter nodded.

Steve stepped up to her. "No mention of home address, school, or any other personal details."

The reporter arched her eyebrows, but nodded.

"Sara's sixteen. That makes her a minor. She's entitled to privacy under the law —"

"I know the law," the reporter replied.

"Then follow it."

Chapter 7

Tuesday was clear and warm. The kind of day when you're not supposed to have a care in the world, Sara thought as she returned to school. From the minute she'd left the scene of the fire, every waking minute had been jammed with the investigation, dinner with her curious and supportive friends, Steve's fraternal concern, and homework. Now came the bustle of classes.

For most of the morning Sara diligently took notes as Mrs. Andrews sat next to her and interpreted lectures into ASL. However, the last period before lunch was a study hall. There was no one to distract her thoughts, no one to keep her occupied, no way to keep out the reality of how terrorizing yesterday morning had been, how close Charlie Gates had come to losing his life.

She tried to get started on a writing assignment, but the image of Charlie's face forced itself into her head over and over. She tried vainly to get some words on her paper, then threw down her pencil. As quickly as possible she asked for a pass to use the library.

Three ninth-graders were in the hall; they whispered and pointed as she passed. Her face burned but she trudged past them and into the school library. Once she was through the doors, she went straight to the periodical shelves for something light, something to fill her mind. The first thing that caught her eye, however, was the morning's *Gazette*.

ARSONIST STRIKES ON REYNOLDS STREET

PASSING TEEN SAVES TERRIFIED CHILD

Below the headlines were two pictures. The first was the charred remains of the back of the Gates's house. The second was a shot of her with Steve in front of Thurston Court.

She had read her own copy of the paper before she'd left for school, but seeing the article on display at school bothered her. She grabbed a rowing magazine and slumped into a chair. She tried to focus on the stories but the print swam under her eyes.

Passing teen. Terrified child. Choking, eye-watering smoke. She began to tremble. Keesha and Liz had been at the Blue Onion; Bret could have been at the city library. The Gates's back porch could have collapsed on her. Charlie's room could have gone up in flames before she'd reached the alley. Tears filled her eyes as she leaned back into the cushion.

She closed her eyes and her mind swirled in a black hole of anger and fear. The impartial curiosity that had kept her riveted to news of the fires had been vaporized by the flames on Reynolds Street. She didn't feel the least bit like a hero. She felt as vulnerable and frustrated as the rest of Radley.

The sudden weight of a hand on her shoulder startled her back to reality. She opened her eyes to find Keesha standing over her.

Tears?

No, she lied. *Tired, that's all.*

Keesha gave her a look that said she knew better.

Okay, more than tired. I can't stop thinking about the fire. Sara looked away, but Keesha bent over to regain her attention.

I know a little bit about how you feel . . . like whoever is doing this is right out on the sidewalk or down the street. Remember I told you that after the fire at the Blue Onion I couldn't sleep for days. I just lay awake and thought about every person sitting at every table. Anger clouded Keesha's expression as she continued. *Was the arsonist there with us? Who hadn't I paid attention to? Who looked demented and evil? Who had a pocket full of matches?*

. . . and a paint can full of rags and gasoline, Sara added. *I'm the one who should feel guilty. Back then I thought of it all like a big, exciting police case, especially since you and Liz were safe.*

Keesha shrugged. *After I left your place last night, I could barely concentrate on my work. I had a terrible night. If only I could have told the police who started the restaurant fire . . . I must have seen him. Liz must have. The Blue Onion isn't that big and we knew half the kids in the place. If I had re-membered something, or could have given your brother some clues, maybe the police would have caught him by now. If they had, nothing would have happened yesterday. You would have come to school, rowed with the team at practice . . . nice normal day.*

Sara smiled sympathetically at Keesha's wide, brown-eyed stare. She pushed herself out of the chair and gave her friend a hug. Then she signed, *Maybe I'm not the only one who should major in criminology when we get to college.*

Two days later Sara borrowed Steve's Jeep to help her crew coach move some new rowing equipment from school to the boathouse. She was home early, in time to walk Tuck to the Penn Street Deli and then over to the police station for dinner with her brother. Eating with Steve at the station broke the loneliness of being in the apartment on the nights when he worked. Since the fire, she hadn't wanted to be alone.

As she entered his small second-floor office, she was surprised to see him limp over from his file cabinet. She laid the hoagies and iced teas on a free corner of his cluttered desk.

Hurt your ankle? she signed.

Steve grimaced. "Broken treadmill." He signed *K, GYM* their name sign for Greg Ketchum, the owner of Ketchum Fitness Center. "I've been trying to support Greg's gym, but it needs a complete overhaul. He took a part-time job with the parks department to make extra money to pay for repairs, but he needs to close the whole operation until it's safe. Sunday night when you were late walking Tuck, I talked to Greg and he agreed. But almost a week has gone by and nothing's changed."

Are you okay?

Yes. He laughed ruefully. "Even with a limp, I'm in better shape than some of Greg's equipment. Speaking of equipment —"

Sara followed his speech and signed, *All delivered.* "Coach Barns says thank you for letting me have the Jeep this afternoon."

Steve smiled as he shoved aside the desk

clutter to make room for the impromptu meal. "I think Dad's old sedan would have worked just as well. That stuff would have fit in the trunk."

"Dad's green clunker isn't a new Jeep." A strong aroma of vanilla drifted through the open window from the Buckeye Foods bakery across the street. Tuck raised his head and sniffed, but stayed in his spot, curled up in the corner.

No smell of ashes and cinders with the cookies this time, Sara signed to her retriever.

"What was all that about?" Steve asked.

"See his nose quiver? Just like Sunday night when he thought I was in danger. He smelled the baking then, too, before the ashes."

Danger, Steve signed. "Too bad you didn't have him with you in the alley."

"Didn't need him. I was okay. I'm still okay."

The article about the Monday fire was pinned on Steve's bulletin board and she watched as he glanced from it to an envelope stuck under his desk phone. Her comment had obviously reminded him of something, but she knew the look and knew better than to ask what was on his mind. "Things are getting back to normal at school," she said instead.

"No one treating you like a hero anymore?"

"No. I even had to make up the biology test." She hesitated, then plowed ahead. "I wish things were back to normal in Radley. Any more clues? Did the lab find fingerprints on the paint can?"

"No. No prints except yours. The squad's working with the Gateses to see if they remember any angry coworkers, anything that ties their fire to the others. But there might not be any tie at all. The fires could be random. The arsonist might just have found convenient places."

Sara shook her head. *No!* *"The house, the restaurant, the library weren't convenient. Just the opposite. If this guy just wants to start random fires, they would all be in places like the garage at the park.* Dexter Sanctuary was empty. Middle of the night, but not the others. Something ties these together."

Steve's annoyed expression made her smile. She signed two words very slowly: *COP; BLOOD.* "I've got detective blood, just like you."

Her brother glowered. "You're not just like me. You're sixteen. Save the detective work for when you've graduated from the Police Academy."

"And I'm old enough so you won't still be my guardian?" *Guardian.*

Despite the tension, Steve managed to smile. *Yes.*

Sara sighed. *"I just want this mess to be over for all of us. No job for Bret."*

Steve frowned and she went back to speech.

"Basketball season is over and Bret was supposed to go back to his part-time job at the library, but his parents won't let him because of the fire there."

"Whoever it is will trip up, sooner or later. He wants the publicity as much as the fires," Steve replied. A small flush started across his cheeks and he gave her a blank look, then changed the subject. "What time is your date with Bret tomorrow night?" he said instead.

"About eight. We might go to a movie."

No movie. Go to a friend's place.

"Liz might have people over," she added, "but we've been waiting to see this film."

Steve signed, *L, RED,* Sara's name sign for Liz. *"Go to Liz's. It's a much better idea."*

"In case the arsonist burns down the movie theater?"

Joke? Not funny.

I know. I'm sorry. I hate everything that's happened. "All I meant was I don't want to be afraid of every place that's open to the public. I can't give in to this. I don't think my friends should, either." She added her voice for emphasis.

"Your friends have the right idea. You can have just as much fun at someone's house or apartment. It's safer to party with friends in your own place."

"You're overreacting."

"Let me decide what overreacting is."

"Steve! By the time they catch the arsonist, the movie will be gone."

"Rent it when it comes out on tape. I want you out of movie theaters for a while."

She sat back in her chair. *How long is a while?*

How long? Steve repeated her sign.

Sara nodded that he'd understood.

"This weekend, for starters. It's been less than a week since the Reynolds Street fire."

"And let the firebug think he's won? Who knows how long it will take to get this guy." Sara raised her eyebrows and punched the air with determined gestures. *"We need to show this guy he can't make us afraid."*

"You can leave that kind of bravery to somebody else," Steve threw back at her.

He was interrupted by Hank Allen, a fellow officer who appeared at the door. The detective nodded to Sara, then winced as he rotated his wrist while he spoke to Steve. Although much of his speech was unclear, Sara caught something about unsafe equipment at the gym. Steve stood up and motioned that he'd be right back. He picked up his sandwich and left the room, as he gave Hank a "follow me" nod of the head.

Sara took a swallow of her iced tea. "And let him think he's won." She'd put her finger right on it. The arsonist was making terror into a game. Whatever he was trying to prove, whatever his own problems were, he was destroying the trust that made Radley such a safe, beautiful place to live.

Not only was the Blue Onion closed, cafés and restaurants all over town had lost business. Her own friends were either afraid or forbidden to hang out in the popular spots throughout the university district. And when would Charlie Gates ever be able to sleep soundly in his own room?

She stared bleakly at the article on the bulletin board and then looked back at the envelope under the phone. She could decipher gestures in a face as easily as her hearing friends detected sarcasm in a voice. Steve had glanced at the envelope as they'd talked about the arson. His expression had told her clearly that there was something in the envelope that had to do with the case. She counted to five.

When she was sure that her brother had gone down the stairs, she pulled it from under the phone. Inside were two identical letters on business-sized paper, and a memo

sheet from the *Gazette* with STEVE HOWELL
CONFIDENTIAL written across the top. It
was enough to make her hands clammy, but
not enough to stop her from reading the letters.

Chapter 8

They were photocopied letters addressed to the editor of the *Radley Gazette*. There was no signature.

> Dear Editor:
> Stick to the facts.
> Pay attention to Detective Howell.
> Any imbecile can see from the
> photograph in your article that he's
> upset about your ridiculous idoliz-
> ing of his sister. The perpetrator is
> out here among us. Readers want
> details on the fires. What clues
> were found at Reynolds Street?

How does Wilkins tie this latest
inferno to the others?
Your newspaper is hardly worth
the paper it's printed on. You're as
bad and sloppy as the television
networks. Don't waste your read-
ers' time by glorifying the exploits
of some schoolgirl who simply
happened along at the time of the
fire. Take a clue from the cop. Forget the girl. Focus on what's important. Sincerely,
A concerned citizen

The second letter was the same, but this
one had a smaller sheet of paper stapled to it.
The typed message read:

Detective Howell:
I thought you might like to see my
letter to the *Gazette*. I could tell by
your expression that you want
your sister out of the news. After
all, it's not her story, is it?

Keep up the good work,
A friend

Take a clue from the cop. A friend. Sara
didn't realize her hands were trembling until
she tried to fold the letters back into the envelope. She finally slipped it under the phone
and looked at the bulletin board. The *Gazette*
article hadn't referred to Steve as a detective.
Steve wasn't even part of this case investigation. The arson squad was a separate divi-
sion. His police work was undercover,
assignments she normally would have considered more dangerous than tracking an arsonist.

She tried to think like her father, like her
brother. There was underlying anger in the
letter, frustration that the focus of the investigation had changed. Obviously the editors at
the *Gazette* thought it was odd enough to
bring it to Steve's attention. She wondered if
they knew he'd already received his own copy.

Her brother returned to the office as she
pushed the half-eaten hoagie around on the
butcher paper.

Problem? he signed.

She lied and shook her head. *Problem for you?*

Steve sighed. "We've decided to try to get a refund on the police memberships at the gym. I feel lousy about it. I knew Greg in college, before he dropped out of the criminology program. I've tried to support the gym, but it's just not safe. I don't have money to waste, and with my undercover work, I can't afford injuries."

Steve continued but Sara could barely concentrate on his lips long enough to read his speech. Someone at the *Gazette* had been concerned enough about the odd letter to give it to the police. How concerned were the police that it focused on her brother? She was sure it hadn't been printed in the paper. Not even her school paper printed unsigned letters.

Who'd take the time to complain in writing that the newspaper had written a single article that hadn't focused on the arsonist? Who would accuse the *Gazette* of being as bad and sloppy as the television networks?

She knew the answer before she finished asking herself the questions. Someone obsessed with all the coverage generated by the fires. Someone who set them.

She glanced at Steve. He'd finished talking and was looking at her oddly. Maybe he'd thought she hadn't understood what he'd been saying. *Sorry about the gym,* she signed to keep him on the subject.

Gym? "I was talking about you staying close to home, out of trouble . . . *so I don't have to worry about you.*" Steve fumbled with his hands and gave up. "Do what I ask, okay? I'm trying to make some time to get our boat in the water before the leaves fall off the trees again. I don't want to worry if I'm out on assignment or at the marina."

Or out with Marisa? She made a cross on her upper arm.

Their name sign *M, HOSPITAL* made Steve flush and Sara smiled. "I'll be careful. You be careful, too."

She finished the visit with questions about the boat and how much work was needed before it could be launched. She would much rather have talked about what really mattered, but for now it would be worse to confess to rifling through his confidential information than to keep her worries to herself.

Chapter 9

The snake in his head was coiled, impatient. The Buckeye River and the empty boathouse glinted under the white moon as he pulled out the third match. That afternoon he'd watched her rowing. Because of her he had to empty and clean another paint can. Had to roll and soak and pack new rags in it. All because of her. The *Gazette* hadn't even printed his letter. Nothing about him. Everything about Sara Howell. He stuffed the article into the trash barrel.

ARSONIST STRIKES ON REYNOLDS STREET

PASSING TEEN SAVES TERRIFIED CHILD

He had another copy in his scrapbook, but it ruined his collection. It was all about her. The snake reared, ready to strike. He dropped the lighted match. Yellow flame ate the newsprint. Steve Howell went first. The protective detective. He laughed. Sara Howell looked up at him from the paper then vanished into ashes.

Chapter 10

Okay, *I'll admit the night turned out better than I thought,* Sara signed to Bret as he walked her from his car into the lobby of Thurston Court.

They'd rented movies and spent the evening at Liz's. The Martinsons' property on fashionable Riverside Drive included an old chauffeur's apartment over the detached garage. They'd updated the apartment for entertaining.

Good. Then ease up on Steve. Your brother's not unreasonable. Everybody's on edge. You saw that tonight at Liz's. Until this guy's caught, I don't think Keesha or anybody else who was at the Blue Onion will go anywhere but somebody's house.

And tomorrow? Sara added, referring to Bret's invitation for the river picnic on his boat after crew practice.

Bret pulled her into a hug and kissed her tenderly. At first he didn't reply. *Are you sure you want to go back to the marina? You've had some awful experiences out there. We could go mountain biking and picnic just as easily.*

If I let that stop me, I'd never leave the apartment. I want to go. I love your boat. It was our first date, remember?

I'll always remember. Besides, it'll be nice to be on the water. It would be pretty tough for an arsonist to set the boat on fire in the middle of the river. Bret hugged her again, then pushed her to arm's length. He cocked his head in question. *Angry about the article?*

Too much about me, and they never should have printed that photograph with Steve in it. They shouldn't be allowed to do that.

Steve was standing next to you.

So what! They should have kept him out of it. Now the arsonist knows who he is. Sara flushed under Bret's scrutiny.

Is Steve in danger? Are you trying to tell me something?

No, she signed, sorry she'd brought up the subject. She wasn't trying to tell Bret anything. At least that much was true. From the moment he'd come into her life, they'd been involved in one terrifying event after another. More than anything else, she wanted him to have no part in any of this. Bret was her safety net.

Often he was the only one who truly understood what she was trying to convey. More than once he'd had to interpret her ASL not only for her friends, but even for Steve. Bret was a friend to confide in, a wonderful guy to date, someone who loved her and would be as angry as her brother if she confessed that she'd read a confidential memo. She and Bret had broken up in the past over issues like this, and she didn't want to think about how painful it would be to lose him now.

Suddenly she couldn't bear the thought. *Are you ever sorry we started dating, after all we've been through?*

He shook his head. *Don't look so serious.*

How could I ever be sorry? You signed your way into my life that day at the library. I'm only sorry it takes so much to slow you down and keep you from getting involved in things that threaten you.

I'm not involved this time. Think about it, Bret. All I did was have C-H-A-R-L-I-E call the fire department and report a fire. Steve and I deserve our privacy. It's the media that's blown it out of proportion. She flushed as she thought about the letter to the editor. She could feel Bret's concerned gaze as he waited for an explanation.

Why do you keep including your brother?

I worry about him. He's all I have. That much was painfully true.

Don't ever forget that you have me, too.

Sara put her arms around his neck and sighed her way into a warm, comfortable hug.

Sara? Bret signed when they finally parted.

She smiled, determined to keep to a safe topic. *Tell me about tomorrow. Can we motor over to Shelter Island for the picnic?*

He smiled. *Any place with you would be perfect.*

Crew practice was at eight in the morning on Saturdays and Sara rolled out of bed at the last minute, glad to see sun streaming through the window as she pulled on her workout clothes. Steve was out walking Tuck, and by the time Sara stepped into the hall outside her apartment, Keesha was waiting.

Keesha pointed to the Howells' copy of the *Gazette*, still on the floor. *Bring the paper with you. There's an article you'll want to see.*

Sara frowned. *Can't. Steve will want it when he gets back with Tuck.*

Then I'll go get ours. Keesha turned to run back into her apartment.

This must be important. News about the fires? Sara asked as Keesha returned and the elevator began its descent.

Keesha shook her head and opened the Young Living section, which highlighted events and people of interest to Radley teenagers and college students. Dread made Sara flush as she looked over Keesha's shoulder.

DEAF TEEN CONTINUES TO MAKE HER

MARK was the headline. This time they'd reprinted a photograph of her with the Radley Academy crew team. The piece was a rehash of the sports article the *Gazette* had run back in the fall, when her crew team had won the medal. Now she'd risked her life, it said. Now she had saved a child. An inspiration . . . a remarkable act of courage for someone who couldn't hear. The mayor had nominated her for a humanitarian award.

Sara sank back against the elevator wall and stayed there until the elevator reached the basement level and the entrance to the parking garage.

This is terrible. She made circles with her middle finger and thumbs, then pushed her hands forward and snapped opened her fingers. *Terrible! Too much about me! They should be concentrating on finding the firebug, not making me into something I'm not. Nobody knows anything more than they did before the fire. I'm no hero. You would have done the same thing if you had been there instead of me. They shouldn't print things like this without asking.*

Keesha stopped short, eyes wide with surprise. *Holy cow, I thought you'd be happy. What's got you so upset? All they did was reprint parts of two old articles.* "You're an inspiration to other deaf kids. The *Gazette* just wants to bring that to everybody's attention. Relax and enjoy the limelight."

Sara frowned as she tried to read Keesha's speech.

"Limelight. Attention," Keesha said. *Enjoy it!*

They started across the garage to the Howells' sedan. "I saved somebody, but I didn't catch the firebug. He's still out there. He's out there, Keesha, watching the TV coverage, reading this stuff —"

"How do you know? Why would he care what's in the paper about you?"

Sara waved at the air, no more willing to divulge what she knew to Keesha than she was to Bret. *That's what cops say. That's what doctors say.* "Psychiatrists study pyromaniacs. It makes sense. If you were angry or crazy enough to set buildings on fire, wouldn't you be interested in the publicity?"

Sara waited for Keesha to nod in agreement, then went back to signing. *I just want things to be normal. At school I want to be treated like everybody else.* "Steve's job is dangerous enough. I don't want to have to worry about stuff like this."

"Stuff like what? The articles?"

Sara's only reply was a disgusted shrug. She angrily fished through her shoulder bag for her keys, then nodded for Keesha to get into the car. She started the ignition, grateful that she had to concentrate on the road and couldn't respond to Keesha's baffled expression.

Crew practice was brisk and demanding. Because she couldn't hear the coxswain who called directions from the stern of the rowing shell, Sara had to concentrate on hand signals she'd devised with her teammates. Out on the river the morning air did little to cool the concern that gnawed at her, but there was no time to think about it. Instead she matched the intensity of Keesha, Liz, and the others who filled her narrow boat. Coach Barns put the whole team through their paces as they

raced over the calm channel along the shoreline of Shelter Island and up into the open
Buckeye River.

When they'd finished the first set of drills,
Sara leaned forward and caught her breath.
She looked downriver at the city skyline with
the sun bouncing off the glistening buildings.
One of the thousands of people in Radley
was out to destroy it. She knew the arson
squad detectives were working nonstop to tie
the Gates family to somebody angry enough
to set a torch to their house, but the fact that
nothing had come up in four days worried
Sara even more. Either the house fire was a
random act of violence or the connection to
the family was so obscure that Robert and
Margaret Gates were unaware of it.

Sara stared at Liz Martinson's red hair as
the team turned the shell around in the river
and headed in the opposite direction. She had
to force herself to concentrate on synchroniz-
ing her oars with her teammates'. With every
stroke, however, she saw either Charlie
Gates at his bedroom window, or the mysteri-
ous letter delivered to the editor of the
Radley Gazette.

From the corner of her eye Sara watched the boathouse slide past, then the tree-covered riverbank where waterside hiking trails and bike paths led to the park at the end. At this hour the only people around were fellow rowers from Radley University or the other high school teams who shared the boathouse. They were concentrating as intensely as she was. Still, she couldn't help feeling that someone was watching her.

Chapter 11

Sara returned to Thurston Court to get ready for her picnic with Bret and found Steve in the living room dressed in jeans and a work shirt. "It's Saturday. I thought you would be at the gym."

Steve shook his head. "I'm on my way to the marina to work on the boat. If we ever want it in the water, I've got to get busy." His shoulders drooped. "I tried to get in my workout this morning while you were at the boathouse . . . give Greg another chance. The gym's still a mess. I don't have enough free time to wait around for equipment he's never going to fix. I asked for my money back."

And the other officers from the station?

He signed, *money,* but frowned at her. "Refund." *Understand?*

Sara nodded and showed him how to sign it. *"They want their money back, too."*

"Right. But I can't worry about that, or about Greg. I've got too many other things on my mind," he added and pointed to the Young Living section of the paper that lay open on the coffee table.

"Keesha showed me the article this morning," Sara replied. Her brother's steady blue-eyed gaze remained fixed on the paper. When he looked up, his handsome face stayed serious. "They completely ignored me when I told them not to publish anything. I don't want anything else in the paper about you." *Nothing more about you.*

Sara crossed the room. *Or you, either. This time they didn't print it, but* —she signed without thinking, then stopped.

Me? Steve's eyebrows shot up in surprise.

Sara felt the heat in her cheeks as she flushed. "Never mind. Go on to the marina. I have to get ready for Bret." She tapped her watch and turned abruptly for her bedroom, but the blush had already given her away. As she hurried down the hall, she could feel the vibrations on the hardwood floors of Steve's footsteps as he came up behind her. She almost cringed in anticipation of his hand on her shoulder.

Instead he came around and stood in front of her, blocking her bedroom door. "What did you mean, 'This time they didn't print it'?" he asked.

Sara sighed. She'd given herself away. *I'm worried about you! Okay, I saw the letter to the editor. It was sitting on your desk.*

"It was sitting under the phone in an envelope!"

"I'm a detective," she tried.

No, I am the detective and your guardian. You are my sister, the one I'm supposed to protect . . . keep safe . . . be a father to. Sara, this isn't the first time you've gone through my files. He raked his hand through his sandy hair in a combination of anger and frustration. "This isn't the first time you've snooped in my office." *When did it happen? The minute I left the room?*

Yes. Amazing, she thought as she finally looked him in the eye. The minute she told the truth, the flush disappeared. Her heart stopped thundering. "It wasn't a file, it was just an envelope." *I know it's no excuse.* "I know how hard the arson squad is working, but I also know they still don't have much in this case. I saw you glance at the envelope and when you talked . . . I knew something important must have been in it."

"Sara, if I had wanted you to know about it, I would have told you."

"You never tell me anything, Steve! It makes me worry more. Don't you know that? Don't you know when I'm here by myself, or at school, or rowing — anyplace — I worry about you as much as you worry about me?"

He gave her a quick hug. *I'm sorry, but that doesn't give you the right —*

"Anyway," she continued, "I thought it would be about the case. I didn't know it would have anything to do with you. Don't be angry. We're on the same side, Steve. I worry for you the way you worry for me." *Understand? I'm not the only one who's wor-*

ried or you wouldn't have the extra copy the editor sent over. It referred to you, not me. How much danger are you in?

None.

"You can't know that. There wasn't much in the letter, but you saw how odd it was. Angry words. This could be from the arsonist and he could be somebody from an old case of yours, somebody with a grudge against you."

As Steve spoke he tried to throw in ASL that he was comfortable with. "It's more likely that the pyromaniac is extremely self-centered, somebody who wants all the attention." *All the attention.* "That's why he started the fires in the first place. The letter was written because the press put all the attention on you instead of him, that's all."

Not all! Sara signed back angrily as she caught his words. *"The letter was about you. He mailed you a copy. The writer knows you're a cop. Cop. You,"* she added in case he needed the extra emphasis. *This person is crazy. Not thinking straight. It's my turn to worry about you, Steve.*

Don't worry! "It won't do any good. Neither will going through my files." It was Steve's turn to flush, and anger brightened his face until his eyes were dark with annoyance.

I'm glad I did, she replied. Between the gestures and the speech, they were on the edge of an argument she knew would get them nowhere. "I have to get ready for the picnic with Bret and you have to work on the boat."

Steve's expression stayed grim. "After your picnic —"

Dinner and movie with Bret.

No movie. "Marisa's coming here for dinner tonight. Invite Bret, too. We'll do something together for a change."

"I know you. You'll sit around and pretend nothing is wrong. You're the one who shouldn't be allowed to go to a movie. The letter was about you, not me." She sidestepped her brother and went into her room.

Her abrupt departure left Steve standing in the hall. It was just as well. They wouldn't resolve anything by standing face-to-face yelling at each other.

* * *

By the time Bret arrived at Thurston Court, Sara had showered and changed into shorts and a striped top. Her damp hair hung loose around her shoulders, but she had barrettes in her pocket to keep it from blowing in her face once they were on the water. She put her favorite flannel shirt in her backpack and headed for the living room.

Steve had left a note saying he'd left for the marina.

I brought something for your scrapbook, Bret signed as he fished through his pocket and handed Sara a copy of the article from the Young Living section.

She touched the fingers of her left hand to her lips and then the palm of her right hand. *Thank you.* Unfortunately her expression was a dead giveaway that she wasn't grateful at all.

Bret arched his eyebrows for an explanation, but Sara opened the door. *Time to get going.*

What was that all about? Bret asked as they left for the elevator.

Nothing.

Come on, Sara. I know you and I know that look.

Sara sighed. *Steve spends all his time worrying about me, but it's time somebody worried about him.*

His undercover work is risky, but I thought you were used to it by now.

Sara looked at her boyfriend. Outside the day was warm and beautiful. There was a promise of a great afternoon together. She wasn't going to ruin it. *His work is hard to get used to, that's all. Besides, we had a fight. He says no movie. He wants us to stay here, have dinner with Marisa and him.*

Fine with me, Bret signed. As the elevator took them to the lobby, he pulled her into a hug and rested his face against her damp hair. *Just like I said before, I'm here, too, if it helps,* he signed as they separated.

Thank you. That's important.

Bret smiled. *You've already spent the morning on the river. This is your last chance to pick another spot. We can still go somewhere else. Don't you ever get tired of it?*

Depends on who I'm with, she signed back

playfully. *It might do everybody in Radley some good just to get out on a picnic and forget about what's been going on — at least for a little while.*

Bret's gaze deepened. *Is that what this is all about? You and Steve arguing over the arsonist?*

Yes.

I knew your problems with Steve were deeper than his just being a detective. They'll find this guy, Sara. Sooner or later all the pieces will fall together or he'll make a mistake and this nightmare will be over.

No one's making progress. The arsonist already made a mistake. He left the paint can at the scene of the last fire and it hasn't helped at all. No fingerprints except mine. No clues to lead the police in a new direction. Nothing!

The elevator opened and Bret put his hand on her arm as they crossed the lobby for the visitors' parking area out front. It was a gesture he'd used a hundred times, and Sara knew what it meant: Stay out of it.

Chapter 12

The route to the marina took them through much of Radley. They passed the museum complex where the parking lot was nearly empty. The park in the city square was full, but there wasn't a soul on the steps of the library directly across from it.

The marina was part of Shadow Point Park and they arrived to find every acre of the municipal grounds alive with activity. The grassy picnic area and meadow was full of kids playing Frisbee and families chasing children. Mountain bikers and runners were on the paths. It was as if everybody in the city had decided that if the library, restaurants, and any other public building could become an arsonist's target at any moment, then they'd all stay outside away from any building where the pyromaniac might strike next.

Bret drove slowly past the picnickers and over to the riverside parking area that served the boaters. At the edge of the Buckeye the docking slips were filled with pleasure boats like Bret's that had either already been launched for the season or were being tuned up and readied for the coming summer.

Sara had resolved to enjoy herself. She smiled as she got out of Bret's car. *I'm lucky to have you. With the hours Steve works, our boat will probably stay in storage half the summer. Look at the docks. There's everybody from kids carrying lunch to mechanics carrying tools.*

No kidding. That's why Dad always puts the boat in early. Even if the weather stays cold, he's ready to go. On a day like this, it'll take till six tonight to get launched or even find somebody from the repair shop who's got time to fix anything.

Nothing needs fixing of yours? Sara signed.

Bret kissed her. *Everything is perfect.*

Sara slung her backpack over her shoulders to keep her hands free for signing. There was a good chance Bret would make her practice her speaking, but with him, signing was fluid and fun and, over the roar of a boat engine, far easier than trying to be understood by speaking.

As she reached for the cooler from the backseat, a man about her brother's age got out of a car just ahead of Bret's. She cocked her head at the vaguely familiar face.

Bret followed her glance and arched his eyebrows to indicate that he wanted an explanation.

She finger-spelled the man's name: *G-R-E-G K-E-T-C-H-U-M*, then showed Bret the sign she and Steve had designed. *He owns Ketchum Fitness Center over by the R-U campus, not far from you. It's no good and Steve quit. He was telling me about it this morning. He feels bad about it, but the equipment isn't safe. Membership renewal is next week, but lots of the detectives who use it agree with Steve.*

Too bad, Bret signed. *Maybe he's going out on the river to forget about his troubles . . . just the way we are.*

Maybe he ought to be back at the gym working. As Sara watched, Greg slammed his car door and hurried toward the storage area. *Look at that. He's not here for the river, he's here for Steve.*

Stop playing detective, Bret replied. *How would he know your brother is out here?*

Steve was at the gym this morning. He probably told him his plans when he complained that he didn't have time to wait around for the equipment to be repaired.

Bret frowned. *Start enjoying the afternoon.*

As soon as we check in with Steve, I will. He wanted us to stop by before we go out on the river. Truth or not, she wanted to see her brother and apologize for their fight. Then she could relax and enjoy herself.

Bret gave her a studied look, but followed as she led the way to their powerboat. It was still up on jacks in the winter storage area. There was a ladder propped against the side and a toolbox open on the pavement. As she approached the bow, Bret suddenly held her arm.

Not a good time, he signed. *Argument.*

Steve and somebody else behind the stern. He pointed to the back of the boat where Sara glimpsed her brother's shoulder.

Is he talking to Ketchum?

Before he could answer, Bret raised his eyebrows in surprise. Greg Ketchum stormed past them, oblivious of their shocked expressions. He spun around once and yelled something in Steve's direction, then continued toward the parking lot.

Sara stood in shocked, embarrassed silence and finally tugged Bret's sleeve. *What was all that about?*

When we arrived, Ketchum was shouting something about Steve being unfair. He said he hasn't given him enough time to make repairs. He's furious about the rest of the officers either not renewing their memberships or asking for refunds. He says he needs the income or the gym will close.

That's all?

Steve told him to calm down. He's sympathetic, but the equipment is unsafe. Bret shook his head. *As he passed us, Greg yelled that it would be Steve's fault if the gym goes under, if he goes bankrupt.*

By the time Bret finished and they reached the boat, Steve was kneeling over his tool-box. Sara knocked on the hull as she approached to get his attention.

Steve looked shaken. "What a day. One problem after another. I thought you two would already be out on the water."

Sara circled her heart. "I wanted to apologize for our fight. Sorry about this one with Greg Ketchum."

"You heard," Steve said to Bret.

"Some of it."

He came by to talk about the memberships. He said the precinct captain was in and canceled the renewals for everybody at the station. Greg accused me of being behind it.

Were you?

Steve shrugged. *The condition of the equipment is to blame, not me.* He wiped his hands on a rag and nodded toward the water. "Sara, I'm sorry about this morning. You two go on out and have a good time. This has nothing to do with you."

I'm sorry. Sorry about everything. Bret and I will have dinner with you and Marisa.

Steve nodded and did his best to look relaxed and forgiving.

Wrong time to get involved in your brother's business, Bret signed once they were headed for the dock. *I can practically see the wheels turning inside your head. Whatever else is on your mind —*

Nothing's on my mind but the river and whatever you packed for us to eat, she signed back, determined to put everything behind her.

Good. Rowing at dawn must give you an appetite. Keep thinking about food. It'll keep your mind off being a detective.

When Sara was settled comfortably next to Bret, he eased the boat out of the slip and motored slowly away from the marina, not increasing his speed until they were out in the middle of the river. The water sparkled. Sara pulled her sunglasses from her backpack and tried to enjoy Bret's riverside tour.

They craned their necks to look up at the houses and condominiums that sat high up on the bluff along Riverside Drive. Kim Roth and Liz Martinson lived on Riverside, and their views of the river were spectacular. Even Liz's garage had a water view. Once they left the residential area, Bret motored down to Radley's business center where the same skyscrapers she had admired that morning seemed to be stacked up alongside each other all the way to the water's edge.

They motored much farther than she had rowed, however, and as Bret took the boat close to the river embankment, Sara frowned at two waterside landmarks. WRAD was painted in huge letters on the side of the television and radio station. Less than a block away the *Radley Gazette* filled an old-fashioned granite building, famous because large windows let the public out on the sidewalk watch the presses run as each edition was printed.

She turned to admire the scenery on the opposite shore, less populated and far less irritating. As usual, Bret seemed to read her thoughts. He smiled sympathetically and steered the boat away from the city, in the direction of Shelter Island, leaving WRAD and the *Gazette* office in their wake.

* * *

Once Bret had nosed the boat up to a sandy opening at the head of the island, he and Sara climbed out onto the woodsy bank that edged the park.

So much for trying to find a private, secluded spot, Bret signed with a laugh. He tapped his ear.

Lots of noise? Sara signed.

From lots of people, Bret replied.

Just beyond the buffer of the trees there was nearly as much activity as there'd been across the river. Sara watched a pair of joggers as they headed for the other end of the island, the end where she'd nearly been drowned in an autumn midnight fiasco.

Thinking about that night last October? Bret signed.

Sara nodded. *I was awfully lucky to have you and Steve there.*

Don't worry about him.

Sara helped carry the basket and cooler and laid out the tablecloth on a private patch of grass with a pleasant view. She leaned against a tree trunk, restless and distracted. When she couldn't stand it any longer, she jumped to her feet. When Bret caught up with her at the river's edge, she punched the air with her gestures. *I love you, Bret. I trust you and I need you, but you have to know what's happened. My worrying has nothing to do with the gym and it's more than just finding the arsonist. It's a letter, Bret, a letter I wasn't supposed to see.*

Chapter 13

Sara waited until Bret was facing her, to be sure he'd get every word. *I feel terrible keeping secrets from you. I'm no good at it. You can always tell when something's bothering me. You need to know what's going on in my life, even if it makes you furious.*

She told him about the letter to the editor, even how she'd found it. Bret didn't argue. He tugged her back to the tablecloth and got her to nibble at the sandwiches he'd packed. The bread stayed dry in her mouth and she finally put it down.

Bret turned to her. *I love you for being honest. I don't want any secrets between us, either, but snooping into your brother's business has never done anything but get you into trouble. This isn't the first time, Sara. I don't want to worry about you every time there's a crime in Radley. I want you safe.*

There's a good chance the letter is from the arsonist himself. It was nothing like what an interested citizen would write. And what does the paper do? It goes and prints another article on me, anyway. The deaf hero.

Bret was already shaking his head. *Slow down, Sara. The story about you was in the back section. There have been plenty of front-page articles about the fires —and the arsonist. You can't expect the press to give in to people who write unsigned letters. You're overreacting because Steve has been stalked in the past by criminals, but don't forget he's a cop. He knows what he's doing. Besides, you told me he has nothing to do with the arson squad. Whoever is out there starting fires and writing letters about it isn't after you or Steve. He's after publicity and making whatever his insane point is. You just stumbled over one of the cases.*

Stumbled over something that's made this whole week miserable.

Suddenly Bret stood up again. *And the*

week's almost over. Let's get off the island. Come back in the boat. We'll move upriver and explore some of the shoreline . . . something that will get our minds off all of this.

Sara was quick to agree. They repacked the cooler, and while Bret got the boat ready, Sara carried their trash to the closest barrel. She paused, about to drop the refuse into the receptacle. It was already half full of burned newspaper, too charred to read. She shuddered at the grim reminder as she looked down at the ashes and then dropped her own paper on top.

Dinner with her brother and Marisa in the apartment wasn't as bad as Sara had expected. Her afternoon cruise, the picnic, and especially her honesty with Bret had finally lifted her mood. As the four of them pulled the meal together in the Howell kitchen, Marisa and Steve flirted with each other. Sara thought about how perfect Marisa was for her brother. She was funny and sweet. Her hours in the hospital's emergency wing made her sympathetic to Steve's erratic hours. She listened to him in ways Sara couldn't, and Sara was sure her brother often asked for advice about raising a teenaged sister.

As Marisa worked on the salad, Steve smiled at her and tried to help. The best part about Marisa Douglas was simply having her in their lives. It gave Steve somebody else to concentrate on.

The four of them ate at the dining-room table, but as soon as they'd finished the ice cream Marisa had brought, Tuck nudged Sara's leg as a reminder that he was ready for his evening walk. She left Marisa and Steve with the dishes while she and Bret took Tuck around the block.

There was plenty of light left in the evening sky and the air was still warm as they pushed open the lobby doors with Tuck between them on his leash. The air smelled of vanilla from the bakery. Tuck led them up the sidewalk, then suddenly froze.

"Not again!" Bret cocked his head. *Fire sirens. Close.*

The firehouse is around the corner, down by Steve's police station. They must be answering a call, Sara replied. *The trucks will*

probably come racing down here any minute.
She and Bret exchanged glances and her
stomach flip-flopped. At this point, she
thought, everybody in Radley must have the
same reaction the minute they hear a fire
truck.

Bret shook his head and frowned. *Sirens
are winding down, like the trucks are stopping. I think they've already arrived at the
fire.*

Bret's ASL made her heart leap. She knew
every store, every inch of the streets between
where she stood and the Buckeye Foods bakery. Other pedestrians turned their heads. Up
at the corner she could see people pointing.

Sara grabbed Bret's arm with one hand
and Tuck's leash with the other. As they hurried along the sidewalk, people started to run.
Sara broke into a jog, too. It didn't matter
that she couldn't hear. Every face on the sidewalk told her something was terribly wrong.
There was still nothing in the air but the
smell of vanilla, but customers were coming
out of shops. The owner of the dry cleaners
had a bundle of shirts in her arms as she

looked up the street. As Sara and Bret reached the traffic light, Bret pulled her to the left and around the corner.

A hook and ladder truck had pulled diagonally across Penn Street. Others were still arriving. Cars went up onto the curb to get out of the way; two of them collided in a fender-bender. The firefighters ran the first extension ladder to the roof in the middle of the block. Light gray smoke drifted into the sky over the chaos as a firefighter moved up the ladder, carrying an ax. A mob of onlookers had formed a blockade making it impossible to see anything but the crowd, the top of the ladder, and the upper stories of Penn Street's stores.

Lieutenant Rosemarie Marino, a familiar face from Steve's station, was the only officer in sight. She looked like she'd run down the street as well. She tried to move the onlookers back to the opposite curb, but at the curb firefighters were working to clear space around the hydrant. Sara stood on her tiptoes and jumped in place as she strained to see over the crowd. Dread made her grip Tuck's leash. All heads were raised, many with hands shielding their eyes.

Can you see which store is burning? she signed to Bret.

Someone pointed and Sara squinted at the roof. The smell of smoke replaced vanilla. Bret dragged her backward across the street and by the time they looked back, the smoke had thickened. It billowed from the windows. Fingers of flames shot out the third floor.

Arcs of water rose from the hoses and smashed against the building. A firefighter climbed a second ladder as it was moved against the wall. The flames were hypnotizing, more brilliant than a sunset, as they heated the air. As the water began to do its work, the smoke thickened to a steamy, gritty blanket that hovered over Penn Street. Sara's eyes watered. Bret wiped his sleeve across his forehead.

An ambulance inched its way down the street and into the crowd. Sara watched the flashing red lights, then turned to follow the EMT's as they pulled open the rear door. They went to assist the drivers of the banged-up cars, but a man on the curb threw his hands over his face. Sara gasped. Rocco Patrone was comforting his brother Emilio.

Not the deli! she signed to Bret. Sara bolted forward and tried to edge her way through the crowd to see for herself as smoke, flames, and now gallons of water destroyed the Penn Street Delicatessen.

Chapter 14

It's the P-A-T-R-O-N-E-S, she signed desperately to Bret. *I can't believe this.*

In the moments Sara and Bret had mingled with the crowd, the street had erupted in chaos. On the other side of the gawking pedestrians, shoppers were still staggering out of the stores or huddled in groups at the curb. Water and debris fell on awnings and people alike. More officers arrived from the station, and a line of squad cars formed a barricade to keep traffic back.

Sara shoved through the crowd toward the Patrones. As she closed in on them, Steve grabbed her by the shoulder.

"Go home right now," her brother said,

inches from her face. He pulled her off the street and into the shelter of a storefront.

She tried to shake off his grasp. "It's the Patrones, Steve! It's Rocco and Emilio. The deli, the apartment —"

"There will be time for the Patrones later. Get back to the apartment. Even if this was only caused by grease in Emilio's frying pan, I don't want you anywhere near the scene of another fire."

"But it's the Patrones!"

As she argued with her brother, the WRAD panel van pulled around the corner. Lieutenant Marino raised her hand and forced it to stop as she waved a second ambulance around it. Although she wouldn't allow the television van any closer than the far end of the block, the newscaster hopped out and shoved through the chaos, with a cameraman right behind her, video equipment propped on his shoulder. They jogged down the middle of Penn Street in search of a human interest angle to yet another fire.

Sara fought her frustration and anger. She wanted to help the Patrones but there was no denying Steve's point. *I'll go. You, too. Come home with me,* she signed. "We all need to go home."

"I can't," he replied and finally dropped his hands from her shoulders. *Needed here. They called me back to work. Here, tonight.* She looked over her shoulder for Bret's support, but her boyfriend had disappeared. *Marisa. Nurse. She'll stay with the ambulances in case there's an emergency.* He crossed his sleeve, the sign for *hospital.*

"Steve —"

"I don't have the time or patience to worry about you. Go home where you'll be safe. I'll be back as soon as I can get away." He tapped his forehead. *Understand?*

Yes, but —

"Find Bret and go home."

Marisa waved frantically. Steve and Sara turned in time to see Emilio clutch his chest and collapse into Rocco Patrone's arms.

Sara grabbed her brother. *Take care of him. Don't let anything more happen.*

Steve nodded. He had to open his wallet and flash his detective shield to get onlookers to move as he pushed toward the ambulance. EMT's slid the stretcher out of the back of the ambulance, but the crowd made the rest impossible to see. The fire captain was barking instructions, still trying to establish order. The flames now leapt from the entire second floor of Emilio Patrone's apartment.

Sara coughed and winced. The air was full of the stench of smoke and ashes. She rubbed her hands over the tears that welled in her eyes. The Patrones didn't have an enemy in the world that she knew of. They were honest, respected. She tried to clear her head of painful memories.

The ambulance light began to whir and blink. Steve closed the doors and said something to the EMT's. Within seconds the ambulance began to make its way slowly through the chaos toward the hospital. Before the crowd closed in again, Sara caught a last glimpse of her brother as he turned his attention to the traffic.

Sara moved away to find Bret and finally spotted him with Keesha's brother Marcus. By the time she and Tuck reached them, Keesha was there, wiping her own tears. Bret pointed to the deli and shook his head.

Just before I ran into Marcus and Keesha,

I saw a kid I used to see in the library: G-E-O-R-G-E B-U-R-K-E-T-T-E. He said he heard it started in the apartment over the deli, not downstairs in the shop. That's why it's so bad — there was nobody in the apartment to hear the smoke alarm.

As if they needed a reminder, flames suddenly shot from the window and curled up the outside wall, then vanished into thick, suffocating smoke as the powerful jets of water blasted from the hoses below.

Sara pressed her stomach against a wave of nausea. *Steve is right. I need to get out of here.* She tugged Tuck's leash and the group began its slow walk back to Thurston Court.

Keesha shuddered and looked at Marcus. "We can't just sit in the apartment and stare at each other. Does anybody want to go over to Liz's? She and Kim rented a movie. It's about the only place Mom and Dad will let me go."

Sara was about to add that Liz Martinson's would be the perfect place to find the support of her friends when Tuck suddenly began to limp.

By the time they rounded the corner, Tuck

had raised his right front paw in an effort to hop. When they stopped, Sara spotted blood on the sidewalk. Marcus and Bret eased Tuck to the curb and lifted his foreleg. With a tissue from her pocket, Sara dabbed it and got the wound clean enough to see that something had sliced deep into the pads of his paw.

"I can't see anything." She ran her index finger over the rough spots. "It feels like something's still buried in his paw. He might need stitches to stop the bleeding."

"Glass?" Keesha said as she signed. *"There was glass out in the street from the cars that collided. He could have stepped on it."*

Sara looked down the block at her apartment building and tried to think. "Bret and Marcus, if you can get Tuck to keep going, walk him home, but wait outside. He'll get blood all over the rug in the lobby. Keesha, will you come with me and call the vet? If I can get an appointment, I'll put Tuck in Steve's Jeep and drive him over."

The small emergency kept Sara's mind occupied. She and Keesha raced into the

Thurston Court lobby and Keesha called Gina Agnew, the Howells' veterinarian. After screening the call, the answering service said to bring the dog in.

Sara thanked Keesha for her help, then smiled weakly at her friend and insisted that she and Marcus get on with their plans. *Go over to Liz's. Bret and I might join you, if this gets straightened out. I could use the company. If not, I'll catch up with you tomorrow.*

Keesha nodded and touched her arm. *If Steve finds out any details about the fire tonight, will you let me know?*

Of course! I'll also call the hospital and get information on Mr. Patrone's condition.

Keesha nodded and looked solemnly at her friend. *You've seen the new sign in the deli window: "Our fortieth year on Penn Street." They just got new curtains and new tables.* Keesha snapped her fingers. *New kitchen in the back, too. Maybe this was an electrical fire. Maybe there was some problem with the new wiring, or maybe it was old wiring. That friend of Bret's said it started upstairs in the apartment. Maybe it was a bad heater or air conditioner . . .*

Sara put her hand on Keesha's arm. *Face it. Maybe the arsonist has a grudge against the deli. Or maybe it was random. He just came across a building that he wanted to burn.*

Keesha's brown eyes were wide and troubled. *Let's hope it was random. Who could be so angry at that wonderful family that they'd do something this terrible?*

Chapter 15

Sara had no answer for Keesha's question. They parted in the lobby. Keesha went back to the boys to tell them that Dr. Agnew would see Tuck. Sara went up to the apartment and got her shoulder bag, the car keys, and an old towel and dishcloth for Tuck's paw. On the off chance that Steve might return before she did, she hastily scribbled out a note.

Sara thought of the Patrone family as she took the elevator back down to the basement parking garage. Forty years. Emilio had to be nearly seventy and now there was the possibility of a heart attack or stroke on top of the fire. She scrubbed her sleeve across her eyes as the doors slid open.

The long, dark corridor from the elevator to the entrance to the garage was the only part of Thurston Court that ever made Sara feel uneasy. Tonight was not a night she would have chosen to walk it by herself. It was barely dusk outside, but down here it could be midnight or noon and the hall never changed its eternal dimly lighted gloom. At the far end there was a glare from the fluorescent ceiling lights in the laundry room and a red glow from the exit sign by the fire stairs. The door to the storage room where tenants rented partitioned areas was shut. The whole corridor was shadowed and smelled of damp laundry.

As the elevator closed behind her, she wished she'd offered Keesha a ride. This place made her acutely aware of her deafness and she could have used a friend with her. Instead, she sidestepped down the corridor with her back to the wall, a trick she'd devised as a child to rid herself of the chills and the feeling that someone was creeping up behind her. The way someone had crept up on Charlie Gates and now probably Emilio and Rocco Patrone, she thought bitterly.

She hurried through the heavy door into the garage. Normally dusk on a Saturday night guaranteed activity in the elevator, down the hall and in the parking area. Tenants would be leaving in their cars for dinner or a party somewhere. Tonight, however, the parking facility was empty. Everyone was still down on Penn Street, she thought glumly, trying to make sense of something that made no sense at all. The green sedan that had been her father's, and Steve's new Jeep were parked side by side in the far corner.

Sara started across the cement floor. She hesitated. A shadow had caught her eye. Her heart jumped in her chest and her pulse raced while she stopped and studied the garage. The heavy industrial columns supporting the ceiling were wide and thick, blocking much of her view. She had the unmistakable feeling that someone was near.

She shook her head and opened her shoulder bag, rifled through the contents to find the car keys, then hurried toward Steve's Jeep. As she rushed, she pressed the car's alarm button on her keychain. The taillights blinked twice to indicate that she'd unlocked the car. Then the garage door slid up, throwing natural light into the entrance.

As Sara glanced over to see who was coming in she accidentally plowed into someone, causing him to fall. He scrambled to his feet and shot out, nearly ramming into the station wagon that was arriving. The person was wearing a knit cap and sunglasses, and was dressed in a dark sweatshirt and black denim jeans. He smelled unmistakably of soot.

Sara ran after him then stopped. The driver of the car was leaning over the backseat fussing with a toddler in a car seat. She didn't see anything, Sara thought as she got into Steve's Jeep to drive around to the lobby.

You didn't see anybody wearing all black run past? Sara signed. Marcus had already gone into the building and Bret eased Tuck into the back of the Jeep. *He was in a ski cap, sunglasses . . .*

Bret shook his head as he placed the towel under Tuck's paw and wrapped the dishcloth over the wound. He climbed in the back next to the dog. *Sara, the garage entrance is on the other side of the building. I told Marcus he didn't have to wait for you, so I had my hands full keeping Tuck still out there. An army regiment could have marched past and I would have missed it.*

You don't seem very upset. Eight o'clock at night and he had on sunglasses. Seventy degrees and he was wearing a knit ski cap.

Bret circled his heart. *I'm sorry. You're right.*

Report it to the doorman. With everybody down at the fire, maybe some guy thought it was the perfect time to steal a car.

I don't think he was after a car. He smelled like the fire — all smoky.

So do you, Sara. So do I.

We're not dressed like we don't want to be recognized! Bret, this could be a break in the case. I should at least describe him to the police. She let her shoulders slump. She couldn't describe him.

Bret pointed to the blood-soaked towel. *Right now we have something else that needs immediate attention. Would you please concentrate on what's important!*

She scowled at the expression on his face

as he signed in sharp, staccato movements. She was about to reply when another car pulled in off the street and waited for them to move. Sara closed the tailgate and left Bret in the back with Tuck.

Dr. Agnew's house and office were near the university's School of Veterinary Medicine, within walking distance of Bret's neighborhood. Sara was tempted to drop him off on the way. There was no denying that she'd gotten herself into serious situations since she'd starting dating him, but she hated it when he lectured her on safety or minding her own business.

She pulled away from the apartment and headed for the veterinarian's office, the opposite direction from the fire. In a few blocks she was lost in thought, glad that Bret was all the way in the back, unable to sign his strong opinions. As she slowed for a yellow light, she glanced to the left, down a long street of row houses. The sidewalks and stoops were dotted with people and the street was lined with parked cars. She hit the brake.

The black-clad man was on the sidewalk on the right side of the street. He wasn't running, but his pace was brisk, hurried, as if he were power-walking to his destination. The bumper-to-bumper line of parked cars made it impossible to get a full view of him, but there was no mistaking the ski cap.

"There he is," she cried. She glanced in her rearview mirror to see if Bret would indicate that he'd heard her. A fraction of a second before the light turned red, she yanked the wheel to the left and shot around the corner, throwing Bret into Tuck. Once she was clear of the intersection, she eased the Jeep to the right, as close to the parked cars as she dared. Slowly she steered down the street toward the departing figure.

When she was less than twenty feet behind him, she realized she had no idea what she'd do when she reached him. For now it would be enough to show Bret. They didn't need to do more than follow him and then she would report it all. They could call from Dr. Agnew's office.

She slowed the Jeep as she slid within inches of the parked cars, grateful there was no one behind her to glare in frustration at her lack of speed. As if Bret had read her mind, he left Tuck in the cargo area and tumbled his way over the seats until he was up front next to her.

What are you doing? he signed angrily as she glanced at him.

"That's him! There, on the right passing the mailbox. I know the hat. The sweatshirt."

Other pedestrians glanced at the Jeep, now nearly at a standstill. Bret broke into impatient ASL. *Stop the car.*

She raised her eyebrows, unable to tell if he wanted to cooperate or argue. "Stop?"

He nodded and she pressed hard on the brake. Bret slid down his window and called something. The man turned around, leaned over as if he were trying to find a clearing through the parked cars, and came back toward them.

Chapter 16

Sara watched in amazement as Bret said something out the window. The man responded. He leaned closer and nodded at her.

"Sara, this is G-E-O-R-G-E B-U-R-K-E-T-T-E, the guy I told you I'd seen at the fire."

You know him!

Yes, from the library.

Sara leaned over Bret and squinted as she tried to read George's lips. He still had his sunglasses on which made it impossible to see his eyes.

"Sorry I slammed into you in the parking garage. I've been to the eye doctor."

As he continued, she lost his conversation and she tapped Bret for a translation. *"He has drops in his eyes. Getting new contact lenses. He says he apologized when he slammed into you. He explained, but he had to run to catch the bus, since he can't drive for the next few hours. He missed it, which is why he's walking home."*

Sara did her best to control her surprise. "You were running through my parking garage." She could tell he didn't understand. Bret repeated it.

"He was at your apartment building to meet the rental agent. He's looking for a new place. The office was deserted. The agent had probably run down to Penn Street to see what had happened. Since he couldn't look at the available apartments, he started to check out the parking garage, but the bus came early."

George stuck his hand through the window and across Bret's chest. Sara reluctantly shook it. Bret continued to speak and sign. He explained Tuck's injury and then nodded and turned to face Sara. *"I offered him a ride as far as the vet's. He lives in the neighborhood."*

Sara glared, but George had already moved to the back and raised the tailgate.

She watched in the rearview mirror as he scrunched in next to Tuck and gave him a pat.

Explain that he's a hearing-ear dog and shouldn't be patted.

Bret looked as irritated with her as she was with George, but he called over his shoulder and then told her to get going. Ten minutes later they were in the parking area in front of Dr. Agnew's office. George thanked them and made his way down the block toward the RU campus.

The minute they were alone, Bret glared at her. *There's enough going on in this city without you playing detective, Sara.*

Did you tell him what I thought?

I said you'd been scared by him in the parking garage.

She stared through the windshield, then turned to her boyfriend. *Since when do you go look at an apartment with drops in your eyes? A Saturday night eye doctor appointment? Get real!*

He said the doctor was a last-minute visit. He didn't want to give up the appointment with the rental agent because it had taken so long to get one.

And you go dressed in black from head to toe?

Sara, if I didn't know this guy, I would be agreeing with you, but I've seen him in black a lot. He's very studious, brainy. N-E-R-D.

Sara drummed her fingers on the steering wheel. *Tell me how you know him. Tell me everything.*

I know him from the city library. He came into my reference section last fall. He was working on a project for college.

He's goes to R U?

Yes. Thousands of students use the library and almost that many wear jeans and sweatshirts. Look around next time you're at the library or we're at the Side Door.

Can't, she signed angrily, hoping he'd catch the sarcasm. *The Side Door Café is off limits now that there's a firebug loose, and you're not even allowed to go back to your job at the library, remember?*

What I remember is that Tuck is in the back with a bloody paw and there's a dog doctor waiting.

Normally Sara would have smiled at Bret's shorthand for veterinarian. Not today.

Not with another tragedy. Nevertheless, she admitted that for now Bret was right. The dog doctor was waiting.

For the second time in a week, Marisa, Steve, Bret, and Sara sat in the Howell den watching a painfully familiar evening newscast. This time it was a live interruption of the regular Saturday night programs.

Tuck was asleep in the corner, still sedated, with his bandaged paw under him. After Dr. Agnew had cleaned out the glass and stitched the wound, neither Bret nor Sara had felt like going to Liz Martinson's. Sara was still lost in thought about George Burkette and irritated enough with Bret that she wouldn't have minded if he'd walked home from the vet's office. His car was at Thurston Court, however, so he drove back with her.

By the time she had driven into the parking garage, he was willing to let her show him where she'd plowed into George.

You're deaf, Sara. He said he apologized and you didn't understand. Maybe he didn't see you.

Deaf, not stupid, Sara replied, then swallowed her frustration, determined to mention the whole episode to Steve as soon as she got the chance. However, Marisa and Steve had returned to the apartment as the news came on and the chance had yet to arrive.

Instead they all sat and stared at the television set. The anchorwoman was standing in the middle of Penn Street, still closed to traffic. The dark street was now deserted and behind her sawhorses and flapping yellow tape cordoned off the Penn Street Deli and the stores on either side. The camera zoomed in on the blackened windows and broken glass that had displayed the gourmet items the delicatessen was famous for. The brand-new red-checked café curtains were now wet, torn fragments. The camera zeroed in on the fortieth-year sign and Sara fought the tears that blurred her vision.

She wiped them quickly so she wouldn't miss the captions running at the bottom of the screen. **Tragedy struck Radley again** was printed out as the anchorwoman spoke. **Behind every one of these blazes there is a story of courage and heartbreak. Tonight's is no exception.**

There were shots of the fire trucks, whirling red lights, blue lights from squad cars, jacketed firefighters, and people huddled on the sidewalk. Sara gasped. The camera cut to a closeup of the entire episode with Emilio Patrone. As Rocco aided his brother and the EMT's burst into action, Steve suddenly appeared on the screen. The camera stayed with him until the ambulance doors were shut and the red light began to spin.

Off-duty officers joined with their colleagues from Radley's fourth precinct to do what they could for the beloved Patrone family. Detective Stephen Howell, whose sister was instrumental in thwarting the Reynolds Street fire just six days ago, was among the officers lending a hand tonight. I've been told by an officer that the Patrone family and the Howell family have had close ties since Detective Howell's father, Lieutenant Paul Howell, saved Emilio's life during a burglary years ago.

She went on to reiterate the death of Paul Howell and then shoved her microphone at the owner of a shoe store from across the street. He agreed that Emilio and Rocco Patrone were beloved and the popular deli was the mainstay of the neighborhood, a favorite of the police officers and firefighters at the nearby stations.

After a final closeup of Steve directing the arrival of an ambulance, the screen went dark and flashed back to the anchorwoman who concluded her report.

Steve, who had been sitting grim-faced on the edge of the couch, stood up and said something to the television Sara couldn't read. He was as flushed as she was pale.

"Face it, Steve, the Howells are Radley's heroes," Bret said. He signed and spoke to ease the tension, but his attempt fell flat.

Chapter 17

Dr. Agnew had suggested that Tuck exercise as little as possible while his paw healed. It was just as well. Sara could barely face the thought of rounding the corner of Penn Street to face the blackened, boarded remains of what had been such a part of her family's life.

The next afternoon as Sara was about to take the week's laundry to the basement, Marisa called from the hospital to report that Emilio's condition had been upgraded. His chest pains had been due to stress, not a heart attack, and after another period of observation, he would be discharged.

Discharged to where? Sara signed angrily to Steve after he relayed Marisa's message.

"I'll find out," he said and went back to his conversation.

Sara took the basket of clothes and left the apartment for the elevator. The Patrones were a large family and she knew he'd be welcomed at the home of one of his children, but that would never make up for the loss, the devastation. She closed her eyes as she rode to the basement. Why the deli? What grudge could someone have against the Patrones?

She wasn't a detective; this wasn't even Steve's case. Nevertheless, the arsonist had struck too close to home. When the library and the Blue Onion had burned, she felt the same alarmed curiosity as the rest of the city, even concern for Bret, Keesha, and Liz. Nevertheless, there had been an element of suspense and unreality about those fires. Now she realized it was as if they had been warning blazes compared to what had followed.

The garage fire at Dexter Sanctuary was an inferno, the first total devastation. And then there was Reynolds Street. If the arsonist knew his targets, Sara prayed that at least he had thought the Gates house would be empty on Monday morning. Charlie Gates's terrified face in his bedroom window was branded in her brain. Now she had watched her brother help Emilio Patrone into an ambulance. It wasn't enough just to be curious, or angry, or frightened. She had to do something.

They were all at risk. If the arsonist could strike at an eleven-year-old boy and a seventy-year-old man, no one was safe. Despite what Bret thought, it wouldn't hurt to have the fire marshall's office question George Burkette. If he was innocent, he had nothing to fear. If he was guilty, the fear in the rest of Radley's citizens would stop.

Sara continued to mull it over in her head as she lugged her laundry basket. She missed Tuck's company as she walked down the long, shadowed hallway. Even he had been affected by the insanity of whoever was terrifying the city.

The laundry room was empty. Sara loaded and started her washing machine. Then she decided to go upstairs, thinking it was worth the extra trip up and down the elevator to get out of the basement. She'd come back when the load was washed and ready for the dryer. As soon as the cycle started, she placed her empty basket on top of the machine and turned for the door. George Burkette was standing in it.

She jumped. He was dressed in another pair of dark jeans and a dark jersey. He couldn't have been more than twenty years old, but he was nearly bald. Okay, she told herself, maybe that's why he wore a ski cap in May. Suddenly she wanted that to be the explanation; she wanted Bret to be right. He was also without his sunglasses and for the first time she could see the intensity in his stare. His eyes were hazel, clear and cold as slate.

Her heart leaped. She expected surprise in his face. Instead he smiled as if he'd been there a while. It didn't soften the hard edge of his glance. As if he were completely at home in the basement laundry room of her apartment building, he leaned casually against the door frame. It blocked her exit.

Tuck, she thought irrationally. If only she'd made Tuck limp down with her. He wasn't anything close to an attack dog, but he was big. Most important, he barked on command.

"Sara, is it? Sara Howell?"

"Yes."

"How is your dog? How's Tuck?" He formed his words deliberately.

Ordinarily she would have been grateful for the consideration, but this wasn't a conversation she wanted to continue. "Fine," she replied. "Not serious."

"Good."

His cold, hazel eyes stayed on her for a long awkward moment. It was impossible to tell if his hesitation came from his uneasiness with her deafness or what he was thinking. She had no way of knowing. As curious as she was, she had no desire to find out.

"I'm here about the apartment," he said finally as he walked toward her. He touched her arm. "Nice safe building. Must be a secure feeling, living with a cop. Your being deaf and all."

She swallowed her surprise at his comment. "Do you know Steve?"

"Only from television. I saw the piece last night on the news. Read a lot about you, too, last week. Sort of runs in the family, I guess, living on the edge, playing hero. I guess the press gets tired of focusing on the firebug. Stories about heroes get better ratings."

In her head the words mimicked the letter to the editor. She rarely missed the sound of a voice. Now she ached to decipher not his words, but his tone. She'd understood everything, but his cold, impassive face made it impossible to tell if he had meant it sarcastically. No sudden hunching of his shoulders or quirky smile gave her a clue.

"Neither of us plays hero."

"Which apartment is yours?" he asked as if she hadn't replied. She continued to read his lips perfectly. The combination of his words and lack of expression chilled her. She answered with a vague, questioning look as if she hadn't understood.

They both turned as a woman in a business suit appeared behind him, out in the hallway. She gestured into the laundry room and George nodded. "This is the rental agent who's giving me the tour."

The agent smiled at him and said something about continuing to look at the storage rooms across the hall.

Sara nodded that she understood, then started to move past him. He touched her arm again. "Maybe we'll be neighbors. With this lunatic running around, it would be nice to have a detective in the building."

Again, she pretended she hadn't understood. Deafness had its advantages.

Chapter 18

Too interested in Steve and me. Too intense. Have you seen him without his sunglasses? Sara could hardly describe the encounter without shivering.

Bret watched her hands intensely as they stood on his patio barbecuing chicken for a quick Sunday evening cookout before another grueling week of school. *Sure I've seen him without sunglasses. He was in the library last fall, remember? He always looks intense.*

Angry?

Bret thought a moment, then shook his head. *He got frustrated easily. If information he was looking for wasn't available ... if somebody else had a book checked out that he needed. But it was more like he was ex-*

tremely focused. Not angry. Bret looked back to the grill as he gathered his thoughts. *Sara, you already knew about his appointment to see the building yesterday. It would make sense that he would show up today. It was just coincidence that you happened to be in the laundry room.* He smiled reassuringly. *If you hadn't had any dirty clothes, you never would have known he was there.*

Which makes me wonder how many times he's been in our building and Steve and I never knew it, she replied too quickly. *And that's another thing. He's a college student, younger than Steve. How can he afford an apartment in Thurston Court?*

Bret shrugged. *Rich parents?*

Sara wrote GEORGE BURKETTE in capital letters and handed the slip of paper to Steve as he dropped her off at school Monday morning. He had been more receptive than Bret, but professional. He reminded Sara that the police had tracked thousands of leads like this one, but agreed to pass all the information over to the arson squad. His biggest concern was George's conversation about the publicity, but in typical detective style he also made her see the coincidences.

Even Sara had to admit the only thing that made her nervous was a sixth sense. "Just a feeling about him," she tried. "Gut instinct. That's what Dad always called it."

"Gut instinct that he's starting fires or lurking around our apartment?"

"Both. Bret saw him on Penn Street, right at the scene. I saw him running through the garage, maybe trying not to get caught. Dressed like he didn't want to be recognized."

"Sara, you told me he had appointments. He has a right to look at a vacant apartment with a rental agent. And you can't tell me anything specific he said about me."

"I'll bet you anything he doesn't move in. He's a student; no income. When Bret and I saw him going home, he had to come up with an excuse for being in the garage, then he made a real appointment just to cover his story."

Steve patted her arm to soothe her frustration. It wasn't frustration, however, it was worry. And it all came back to instinct. Gut instinct. She opened the Jeep door and thanked him for dropping her off. "Steve, you always worry about me. Want me safe, out of trouble. Well, now I'm worried about you. Maybe he's connected to some old case of yours. Maybe —"

Her brother pointed at the Radley Academy building. *"Enough maybes. Worry about school. I'm fine."* He thumped his heart. "Right now I'm concerned about Emilio and what's to be done for him. His building is a total loss. He's devastated."

"If George Burkette did it, he needs to be put away."

I won't argue with that. You're right.

She knew by the look in his eye and the haste in his hands that his signing was just to make her happy. At that moment she missed her father with an ache that was bone deep.

An English quiz and new long-term assignment in history kept Sara focused through most of the day, but as she rushed past the announcement and message bulletin board, she was surprised to see her name on a piece of school stationery. She entered her biology class as she opened the note from Brenda Fletcher.

> Sara,
> Steve called with a message about this afternoon. Please stop by my office before you leave for crew practice after school.
> Thanks,
> Mrs. Fletcher

Thoroughly confused, Sara read it over twice before putting it in her shoulder bag. Something important enough for him to call the school had interrupted her brother's day. Not only that, rather than follow normal procedure and call the Upper School office, he had sought out a friend of the family.

Sara's stomach stayed in knots through the class. Even with her interpreter beside her, Sara had to force herself back to the subject at hand. Again and again she imagined Steve with a crucial discovery about Burkette or some other lead in the case — something that was vitally important.

What on earth is on your mind, girl? Keesha signed with a few quick gestures as the bell rang and classes changed.

Come with me to your mother's office so I can find out, Sara replied, ignoring Keesha's surprised expression. Once they reached the office, Sara expected to be led in and the door closed. Her palms were damp as Keesha's mother waved a greeting.

Instead Mrs. Fletcher smiled. "Steve called. He wants you to make a delivery to the marina on your way home from crew practice, since it's the same direction. It seems Rocco Patrone asked Steve for help getting Emilio settled at his son Anthony's house in the West End. Steve was supposed to deliver oil filters and gasoline to the mechanic at the marina for your boat. Steve said he would leave the Jeep for you in the regular parking spot in the garage. It's all packed, just swing by the boatyard and drop the stuff off. The mechanic is expecting you at the repair shed. He said you knew where to go."

Mrs. Fletcher looked at Keesha who often translated.

Sara nodded. "I got it. That was all?"

Mrs. Fletcher raised her eyebrows and smiled. "Isn't that complicated enough? Steve wanted to make sure I explained it all personally. He also wanted to give me the good news about Emilio. We've all been so concerned about him."

"Did he say anything else about the arsonist?"

"Heavens no. Does he have some new information?"

Sara shook her head. "I guess not."

Relieved that there was no emergency, Sara and Keesha changed into their workout clothes with the team, but explained the errand to Coach Barns and hitched a ride to Thurston Court from Kim Roth who dropped them at the garage entrance. As the door slid up, Sara glanced inside at the structural column where she had knocked into George Burkette. So far she hadn't mentioned him to Keesha. She planned to, once they weren't so rushed. She'd learned from the two times she'd tried so far that her theories, fears, and descriptions took time and patience to convey.

As she pressed the button on her keychain to unlock the car, Sara checked the Jeep's rear compartment and smiled. Steve had laid out an old blanket under the red plastic five-gallon safety container of gasoline and the can of motor oil.

My brother treats this car better than he treats the furniture in our apartment, she signed to Keesha after she pointed through the rear window. *It's a good thing Tuck didn't get blood on anything Saturday.*

Keesha laughed and tapped her watch to indicate that they shouldn't keep the team waiting as Sara got into the car.

The brief humor faded as Sara drove the Jeep onto the street and stopped at the traffic light. Halfway down Penn Street was the bleak reminder of why Steve couldn't make the delivery himself. It didn't matter how many times she passed it. Emilio and Rocco Patrone's gourmet delicatessen and grocery was a blackened shell, cordoned off even to salvage and restoration companies until the fire marshall finished the latest investigation. It broke her heart.

Unconsciously Sara gunned the engine and picked up speed, anxious to get away from the horrible reminder. They headed back past school and along the busy streets that led to the river. Just as she merged with the heavy traffic heading out of Radley on the Tenth Street Bridge, Keesha tapped her shoulder gently.

Sara glanced at her quickly and started over the river, surprised at the apologetic expression on her face.

Sorry. There's noise coming from somewhere up here, Keesha signed.

Sara had to look back at the bridge. "Under the hood?" she asked as the Jeep jostled over the potholes.

Keesha leaned forward so Sara could see her and nodded.

They were fifty feet above the Buckeye on the old bridge that was nothing but pavement — two lanes wide — hemmed in by iron railings. There was no shoulder and no way to stop without creating a massive traffic jam behind her.

Keesha tapped the windshield. She was either pointing to the hood of the Jeep or to the boathouse, below them on Shelter Island.

"What?" Sara blurted. "What do you mean?"

Island, Keesha signed by sticking her hands in front of Sara. *I think we'll make it. Drive to the island. Then stop.*

Island, Sara thought with relief. The noise can't be that bad. She left the traffic and steered off the exit ramp, down onto the familiar street that ran the length of the island from the park's picnic areas to the boathouses. She increased her speed, anxious to get to the parking lot. Suddenly Keesha tapped her arm again. This time it was hard.

Sara turned her head as far as she dared. Keesha looked concerned and she tapped the windshield, then her own ear. *"Noise is louder. Engine?"*

Sara gripped the wheel. It didn't matter that she couldn't hear anything. She could smell. Her nostrils flared at the sudden uncharacteristic odor of hot oil and burning wires.

She tapped her nose and Keesha nodded that she smelled it, too. She pointed again, this time through the windshield to the boathouse parking lot. *We're almost there.*

Sara sped up. Immediately smoke oozed from the hood up over the windshield. She yanked the steering wheel to the left, swerved across the lane and slammed on the brake, sending both of them against their seat belts then back as the Jeep skidded to a stop on the shoulder of the road.

"The car's on fire!"

It's the whole car! Keesha signed before frantically unhooking her seatbelt.

Sara had no time to think. Keesha pounded her shoulder and shoved her into action. Sara got out of her belt as flames shot up outside Keesha's passenger-side window.

"Gas! In the back!"

They rolled, one on top of the other, out Sara's side of the car, then scrambled to their feet and ran. Fifty yards ahead of them in the parking lot, teams from Radley's high schools were assembled with their coaches.

Sara and Keesha screamed and waved them back. As they reached the group Sara turned around in time to see flames engulf the Jeep. Fire wrapped the side, licking up from underneath the chassis and inside the hood. In a blinding flash of orange and yellow heat, the entire vehicle exploded.

Chapter 19

Sara screamed. Her throat was raw but she didn't know — didn't care — if anyone had heard it. She looked from Keesha's terrified expression back to the inferno that had been her brother's prize possession. Without thinking she started forward only to be stopped in midair as two boys from the team threw their arms around her waist and lifted her off her feet.

"Don't get any closer," one of them said.

Coach Barns was gasping and every team member, from Liz Martinson to the kids she hardly knew, stood rooted to the ground as the car continued to blaze.

* * *

By the time the police and fire trucks made it through late afternoon traffic and onto Shelter Island, the Jeep was a total loss. The police officer who took down the information raised his eyebrow when Sara gave him her name.

"Howell?"

She nodded. "The Jeep was registered to my brother Stephen. I think I should talk to somebody on the arson squad."

Unlike the small, familiar quarters of the fourth-precinct police station, there was nothing welcoming about the downtown detective bureau. Even though Sara had been there after the Reynolds Street fire, it was still a blur, as if she'd tried to block out the memory of a week ago. Downstairs in the lobby, as she and Keesha waited for the elevator, Sara had looked at the portraits of firefighters and police officers who had died in the line of duty.

Lieutenant Paul Howell's picture hung in the entrance hall, just as it did in the Penn Street station, but that only deepened her depression. The curious child on a visit with her detective father was gone. He was gone. She was in the middle of a catastrophic situation and she had to think like an adult.

As she and Keesha sat down at the conference table, Keesha began to shake, as if the shock of her near miss had just hit her. The police officer in charge got them both glasses of water. He tried to act casual as he mentioned that members of the arson squad would join them. "There's no reason to think this is related," he added. "But after your publicity last week, Sara, it's just a precaution . . . after everything that's happened lately."

Sara shook her head. "It was Steve's car and he was supposed to be driving it. It was a last-minute change." She did her best not to tremble.

The officers took notes and taped every word. Keesha did most of the speaking as she and Sara were asked to recall even the most innocuous detail from the moment they entered the parking garage at Thurston Court to their terrifying ordeal at the boathouse parking lot. Keesha described the sound and the smell of heat and where she'd first glimpsed the smoke, until she was exhausted.

Sara looked from one impassive face to another. Notes, notes, notes. This case file could probably fill a room. They were polite, attentive — and skeptical. Nothing in any officer's expressions or body language said they considered faulty wiring and engine failure connected to the torching of buildings.

Sara swallowed. Maybe she wouldn't either, if it hadn't been her brother's car. "You should know about George Burkette," she blurted. She wrote down the name and as clearly as possible explained reading the letter to the editor she had found on Steve's desk.

"You think Burkette might have written it?"

"I don't know. He spoke to me about the same issues, about Steve being a detective. Same tone. It wasn't what he said as much as the way he said it. Same things bothered him that were mentioned in the letter."

She regretted it the minute she spoke. The officers had been straining to understand her and now they exchanged dubious glances. She couldn't hear. She was deaf. How could she possibly have picked up anything but straight dialogue from the conversation?

Sara leaned forward. "I watch people when they talk." *Watch,* she signed then rotated her wrist to turn the word to *"See. I see things you don't when someone speaks. Eyebrows, a squint —"* She dropped her hands. "What's important is the fact that if he's the arsonist maybe he's been hanging around Penn Street watching Steve. He would see Steve in the Jeep; he'd see the Jeep at the station. Saturday he saw Steve's parking space at our apartment. He knew where the car was kept."

The officers didn't appear any more convinced than Bret had been.

As Sara finished, her brother rushed into the room with the officer who had picked him up at Anthony Patrone's. Steve was flushed and wide-eyed as he fought his anger. It was the first time Sara had seen him so upset. He demanded details and waited while the fire marshall was called from his office.

Ed Wilkins arrived with a file of papers

and told Steve the burned hulk of the Jeep had already been impounded. Sara's heart raced painfully as she thought of the specialists going over every inch of the charred chassis for clues. He shook his head at a question Sara couldn't read. No, he explained, they didn't have a shred of evidence yet that the Jeep fire had anything to do with more than faulty wiring in the engine. They would, however, talk with George Burkette as Sara had suggested. They had a policy of following every tip they received.

Steve shot Sara look of surprise.

Ten minutes later Sara leaned back in her seat and tried to keep her eyes closed. Keesha's father had picked them up and he and Steve were deep in conversation in the front as they headed back to Thurston Court. Keesha explained that they were talking about Emilio Patrone and started to interpret, but Sara shook her head. She welcomed the blackness that plunged her into isolation. No sight. No hearing. Sometimes it was soothing and gave her time to think, but now her mind was reeling.

Before they had left the conference room, Steve had demanded that if the media got wind of the Jeep fire it was to be reported as a simple mechanical failure. Since the Jeep was being driven by minors at the time of the incident, no names would be released.

That will keep us out of the late news, Sara thought bitterly. She opened her eyes and watched the city streets pass just to keep her mind occupied.

Steve was still deep in conversation with John Fletcher when they finally got off the elevator and walked to their separate apartments. Brenda Fletcher threw open her door and pulled Keesha into a hug. Steve reassured both of them that Keesha was safe, just an innocent bystander. There was no evidence that the car had been sabotaged, he repeated. Innocent bystanders or not, Sara and Keesha could have been on the bridge when the car caught fire. They could have been trapped in traffic, unable to get out so easily.

Steve unlocked their own apartment to Tuck, whose dinner was long overdue. Sara followed her brother into the kitchen and filled the water dish as Steve mixed kibble and opened a can of dog food.

"If someone else's car had caught fire, would the police be as interested?" she asked as he put the dish on the floor.

He nodded. *Of course. They're trying to pull this all together.*

Her stomach knotted as Steve's expression confirmed what she'd been afraid to think about. "That's it, isn't it?"

Steve tapped his temple to indicate that he didn't understand. She was sure that he did.

She raised her eyebrows. "It isn't just anybody's car, Steve." She added ASL for emphasis. "*It's your car. First there are fires at a library, restaurant, storage garage, and a house. The police have proof that the same person started each one. They just don't know why yet, they don't know what connects them —*"

Sara, stay out of this, Steve began.

Sara brushed away his hands. "It's too late to stay out. *Too late! You know I read that letter to the editor. You think it's from the arsonist and it mentions details about you that weren't in the paper. Ever since Saturday*

I've been asking myself why the deli? Why was it the next target? What is the connection to the garage, the Blue Onion, the G-A-T-E-S house? I got my answer this afternoon."

Sara, that's enough!

She shook her head. "You can't keep me any safer than I can keep you. The firebug wasn't after the Patrones, he's after you. And this afternoon proves it."

Chapter 20

"This afternoon doesn't prove anything except that the Jeep had wiring problems and I had put a full gas can in the back."

"There's more to it. Face it, Steve. First I get my name splashed all over the papers for the Reynolds Street fire. Then you get a warning to keep me out of the news. The *Gazette* goes ahead and prints another story about me. Don't you see? Obviously the arsonist doesn't think straight. In his mind you ignored his warning. He got even with you just the way he got even with his other victims."

"Sara, you don't know a thing about the connection to the others. It's all still under investigation. Leave this to the professionals."

"You just admitted that they haven't come up with anything. I have. Suppose the arsonist has been watching or following you. He'd see you go into the deli almost every day. To get information he gets friendly with the Patrones when they wait on him. You know how they love to talk with their customers. What if the arsonist went into the store after you and pretended to know you?"

Steve tapped his ear, at a loss to follow what she was saying.

Sara pushed her open right hand forward into a fist and hit the raised index finger of her left hand. *Pretend. Pretend to know you to get information from Emilio.* She acted out the scenario. "The arsonist orders a sandwich. When Emilio gives it to him the firebug says, 'Thanks. Wasn't that Steve Howell who just left?' Emilio brags about you like always, Steve. You know how he is. 'Yes, that was Steve Howell. He's a cop at the station just up the street. He'll be a great detective like his father. His father saved my life. Steve's like my own family.'"

Sara paused. The flush across her brother's

cheeks told her not only that he was following her speech, but that she had struck a nerve. *"You know what I'm going to say, Steve. The arsonist now knows how important the deli is to you. More than a shop for lunch or dinner. More like family. He needs to get even with you."* Her hands began to tremble. *"He doesn't care about the Patrones. It's you, Steve. He destroys something you care about."*

By the time she finished, the flush in Steve's complexion had drained to paste. His lips were a thin, tight line. As awful as it was, it could very well be true and Steve knew it.

"There's more. We know from the letter to the editor that he loves publicity. We know he's already upset that the press didn't focus on him after Reynolds Street. He burns the deli and what happens? All the local heroes on Penn Street make the news. You make the news." She pushed her hair from her eyes. "Maybe I'm wrong." *I hope I'm wrong, but now he's so crazy and angry that he wires your car to catch fire. You know this isn't co-*

incidence. You know the police will find evidence."

Don't know, Steve signed back angrily. "Sara, I don't know any such thing. It could have been an electrical problem."

"A problem set up by the arsonist," she threw right back at him. *"It wasn't just anybody's car, Steve. Not mine. Yours."* Her own words terrified her and she swiped at the tears forming in her lashes. *"He wouldn't have known I would be driving it this afternoon. It was wired to burn with you in it. Don't you see? Murder. Your murder. Get the arson squad to question B-U-R-K-E-T-T-E. Bret knows him from the library. He was at the scene of the deli fire. He's been snooping around our building."*

"That's just your interpretation. You can't pin something this big on a guy just because he was in the wrong place at the wrong time."

"It was the right time." *Right time!* "It might be the clues that break this case." *And save your life,* she added in sign, even though she knew he didn't understand. Before Steve could respond, she threw her arms around his neck and hugged him for all she was worth.

Sara and Steve ate dinner with the Fletchers but no one had much of an appetite. Brenda and John asked to be informed not only of any news from the police, but also of Steve and Sara's schedules. After dinner, however, there was still homework and business to take care of, so the Howells crossed the hall to their own apartment.

Steve went into the den to call their insurance agent and report the Jeep fire. The minute he finished, Sara called Bret on her TTY. Depending on their school schedules, days often went by during the week when her only contact with him was through the machine. Even if the media didn't find out about the Jeep fire, Penham School had a crew team, too. Anyone who had been at the boathouse would be describing the inferno. In the morning rumors would fly at Bret's school as well as hers. She typed out a quick, succinct message explaining everything before he learned about it from someone else.

She was thrilled when Bret insisted on picking her up the next afternoon after practice.

Sara was bleary-eyed at breakfast. Sleep had consisted of fitful dreams, visions of fires, and Charlie Gates's window. It wasn't Charlie she saw at the window, though. In the nightmare it was Steve behind the glass, trapped.

At breakfast she wrestled a promise from her brother that he would tell her his schedule and keep her informed of any leads or developments. He also explained that he intended to get back to his normal work routine. For once she welcomed the fact that he was out on undercover assignments. It might make him tougher to track.

School dragged. How was she supposed to concentrate on subjects as meaningless as history and English when her brother's life was in danger? Sara fidgeted through the day with her stomach in knots and her head in the grip of a pounding headache.

In study hall she laid out her books and paper and did her best to immerse herself in homework, but within minutes she was staring unfocused at the blank notebook. Her nerves were raw. She wanted to be on the street, tracking George Burkette. She wiped her sweaty palms on her school uniform and wrote his name in block letters at the top of the page.

An arsonist probably had an unlisted phone number. However there were other ways to find his address. He would be registered with the Admissions Office at the university; it took a mailing address to get a library card; he'd mentioned a car which meant the Department of Motor Vehicles would have him listed, as well. Sara drummed the table, then wrote LIBRARY CARD and circled it.

Sara looked out the window. GEORGE BURKETTE. Was he in class right now? Was he sitting with an open notebook somewhere on the RU campus plotting his next inferno? What was left to do after wiring a car to explode? She knew the answer. She pressed her fingertips against her temples and tried to get rid of the headache. Maybe Burkette was on the street right now, following Steve, getting closer and closer to his final act of revenge.

Chapter 21

If it were that easy, the police would have caught him long ago, Bret signed to Sara as they walked along the jogging trail after crew practice that afternoon.

He wasn't a suspect long ago. He isn't one now, Sara signed back. *You should have seen their faces at the station yesterday when I tried to get them to take this seriously.* She grimaced at Bret's expression. It was full of sympathy — for the arson squad. She turned and watched rush-hour traffic move along the bridge over the Buckeye River. Crew team members joined the steady stream of cars as they left the island and headed home.

He needs a name sign, Sara added. She

opened her fingers and made the wide circular motions for fire. *G, FIRE.*

Bret's expression clouded. *That's right, fire. You're in the midst of something extremely dangerous. And you'll try to solve this yourself.*

I'm trying to save my brother, Sara replied as she ground her sneaker into the gravel. *This isn't just some case I'm curious about. I want the police to investigate. If they won't, you can get his address for me. There's nothing dangerous in that. You could invent some reason to have a librarian pull his address out of the computer. You worked at the library; they'd trust you.*

You want me to lie and get you more involved than you already are? Let the police do their job. Bret angrily made a fist and pulled it down from his mouth: *PATIENCE.*

This is no time for patience, not if my brother's life is in danger.

Sara turned and stared at the river. Who was she kidding? Bret would never help her with something so dangerous. He'd lecture and argue and insist that it was for the police to handle. She sighed. It was time to end the conversation before they got into an unresolvable argument.

Bret tapped her shoulder. *Has Steve had time to decide what to do about the Jeep?* he signed abruptly, as if he'd read her mind and agreed completely. It was time for a safe, neutral subject.

Sara shook her head. *Insurance will replace it, but there's lots of paperwork. He loved that car.*

And I love you, Sara. We've already been through so much together — too much. Leave this to the professionals. Give them time to discover it was just a faulty engine. Wait for the crime lab results.

Believe me, I don't want to be any more involved in this nightmare than you do. I have better things to think about. To prove it, she put her arms around him and kissed him. Being close to Bret always made her feel secure, but even with the low sun sparkling on the river and the warm weather she was chilled to the bone. *But in this one case I can't help but be interested. It's too close to me now.*

Sara was right about George Burkette's phone number being unlisted. When she dialed information on her TTY, and typed in his name, the operator typed back the reply Sara expected: Unlisted at the customer's request.

More questions filled her head. Why would a twenty-year-old not want to be reached easily? The only person she knew with an unlisted number was Kim Roth, but the Roths had good reason.

Kim had been kidnapped in the fall. George Burkette must have a good reason, she thought, and somebody had better find out what it is. Patience, Bret had signed to her. It was what she had the least of.

The following night, she stood in the den in the middle of an argument with Steve. "Why haven't the police called? They said they would talk to him." *G, FIRE,* she showed Steve the name sign. "He has an unlisted number."

Steve raised his eyebrows. *Leave this to the squad!*

All I did was call the operator.

The phone rang and for once her brother's expression changed from frustration to curiosity as he listened, nodded, and finally hung up.

Police? she signed.

Yes. They talked to Burkette. They talked to the parks department and they talked to the director of the city library.

Sara's adrenaline began to pump.

"He never worked for the parks department; never worked at the library or had a fight with anyone there. He has no account with Robert Gates's bank and Gates didn't recognize his picture. Neither did Emilio, Rocco, or the owner of the Blue Onion who was working the afternoon of the fire."

Sara flushed. "They checked all that?"

Steve pointed to her embarrassed expression. "Did you think the squad wouldn't put in that kind of effort? Do you know how many of these kinds of leads they've had to follow? How many dead ends they run into?"

Sara circled her heart.

Okay, you're sorry. He relaxed a little. *I know you're worried for me.* "I'll admit they do think the arsonist was trying to send me a message." Steve paused and walked to the window. He stared even though the curtains were drawn. When he turned around to face her, his jaw was clenched.

What is it? Something about the Jeep?

"The lab found traces of an incendiary device." He tapped his temple to ask if she understood. "Wires to a mechanism that caused the fire. Set off by the heat of the engine."

Sara sank to the couch. "You mean as the car ran, the heat from the engine lit a fuse?"

"Sort of."

"Somebody had to know where your Jeep was parked in order to put this device in it."

Steve nodded and for a long moment they stood and looked at each other.

Chapter 22

The moment was broken by Tuck who limped in and nudged Sara's leg. At the same time Steve turned toward the foyer.

Doorbell, they both signed.

Steve brought Greg Ketchum into the den, but he refused a seat. Instead he paced from the couch to the bookcase and back. "Sorry," Sara watched him say. "I came to say I'm sorry."

She offered to get him a soda but he shook his head.

"This isn't a friendly visit, but I do need to apologize. I lost it at the marina last Saturday."

Sara frowned and looked at Steve for a translation. *He got angry,* Steve signed.

Sara nodded that she understood.

Greg pointed at her. "You and your boyfriend even heard it." He stopped suddenly and blushed at his blunder.

Sara smiled and tried to cheer him up. She tapped her ear. "Don't worry about me. Deaf, didn't hear a thing."

"Well your friend sure heard me. And Steve, too. I've got a short temper and, Steve, I don't need to tell you how much pressure I've been under."

Steve leaned against the desk. "Look, I understand. I feel terrible about quitting the gym, but I can't risk an injury and you can't risk a lawsuit from somebody who won't be as understanding as I am. For your own good —"

Greg scowled and thrust an envelope at him. "Don't tell me what's for my own good. You and your buddies quit for *your* own good. I need time. The bank won't give me another loan until I clean up my credit. All I'm asking is for you to take your membership back. Free for six months. You don't even have to use it, just tell the guys at the precinct station you're giving me another chance. They're the backbone of my memberships."

Sara grew more and more uncomfortable as the discussion continued, but Greg stood between her and the door.

Steve's expression was full of regret. "Greg, it's been a long, horrible few weeks. I've got more important things on my mind —" He flushed. "You know what I mean." He touched Greg's shoulder apologetically, but Greg shook him off.

"You mean the fact that I'll lose everything if the gym goes under isn't important, even though you could —"

"Of course it's important. Nobody wants you to fail, but . . ."

Conflict showed in Steve's face, but as Sara glanced at her brother, Greg stepped away from the door and she decided it was a good time for her to leave.

The weather changed. Storm clouds formed and the temperature dropped. Spring rains replaced the sun for the rest of the school week.

"The arsonist will have to work harder in this weather," Keesha joked in the cafeteria as she and Sara joined their friends, but nobody laughed.

No matter what his shift, Steve was now picked up and delivered from the police station by Lieutenant Marino, Marisa, or another officer. He tried to use the destroyed Jeep as the explanation, but their sedan was in the garage and the police station was within walking distance. Sara knew that someone with authority had insisted on the escort.

Knowing her brother was under even an informal surveillance soothed her nerves, but she was still wound tight as a spring. During the next week Steve and Sara talked about replacing the Jeep when the insurance company made the settlement. They invited Emilio Patrone to dinner, but his son reported that he was still too depressed. The fire marshall held a press conference to announce that the destruction of the Penn Street Delicatessen fit the MO of the earlier fires. Remnants of kitchen matches and traces of gasoline-soaked rags had been found in the charred remains of the apartment kitchen. Demolition began on the building.

After crew practice on Thursday, Dr. Agnew removed Tuck's sutures. The retriever emerged from the veterinarian's office with barely a limp, anxious for exercise.

Sara ruffled his fur and snapped on his leash. *Who can resist a girl and her dog?* she joked as she started toward Bret's, hoping a surprise visit would improve things between them.

The neighborhood was bustling with university students in their last weeks of the semester. Sara scanned the unfamiliar faces as if George Burkette might suddenly appear.

The window of the store she was passing brought her back to reality. KETCHUM FITNESS CENTER was neatly printed on the plate glass. She caught a glimpse of Greg Ketchum behind a desk in the corner. Two people were riding stationary bicycles. The rest of the equipment stood idle.

Steve had told her Greg had set up the equipment in full view of the street to generate publicity and interest. It didn't seem to have worked. It was early evening, and the gym should have been packed. No wonder Greg wanted the officers in there.

A few days after Greg's visit, Steve had turned down his offer. Steve had tried to explain how hypocritical it would make him if he accepted a free membership, especially if he didn't use it for safety reasons. It had led to another argument. Sara shook her head in sympathy with her brother. The decision couldn't have been easy.

By the time Sara reached the Sandersons' house, she was more depressed than ever. Bret read it in her expression as he pushed open the front door.

Nice surprise. You look like you need a major dose of cheering up. For starters he pulled her into a warm hug and kissed her.

It's the weather, she signed, then pointed to the overcast skies.

Bret scoffed. *I know you. It's never as simple as the weather. There haven't been any more fires. You've told me Steve is safe. No threats. No problems . . .*

Maybe there haven't been any more prob-

lems because the police questioned Burkette. Now he knows the police know who he is. Makes him nervous.

If George Burkette is the arsonist, I don't think the police want him nervous.

His words and the set of Bret's mouth made Sara's heart leap.

Chapter 23

Rowing helped Sara's restlessness, but it was a team sport, and it was only available after school. The rest of her friends were as edgy as she was. When Sara suggested they go biking, everyone jumped at the idea.

Saturday the weather cooperated and they decided to tour Riverside Drive and its wooded paths above the river. Sara and Keesha pedaled to Bret's to pick up Bret and his friend Damon Miner. They met the rest of the group at Liz Martinson's.

In the weeks since the fire at the Blue Onion, Liz's converted chauffeur's apartment had become so popular as a safe place to hang out, they referred to it as The Garage. Bret and Sara combined Liz's name sign

L, RED with *GARAGE* to come up with gestures that everyone knew meant the comfortable rooms over the Martinsons' garage.

The wind in her face, the views of the river, and the company of her friends was exactly what Sara needed. By the time they returned to the Martinsons' at four, it had started to drizzle. They were too muddy to go inside, but they were exhilarated. Liz suggested that they regroup in a few hours and order pizza. Kim Roth agreed to rent a couple of movies.

In a light rain, Sara biked back to Thurston Court with Keesha, anxious for a shower before Damon and Bret returned for them at six o'clock. She hadn't felt this relaxed in weeks. She smiled at Keesha. "That was the first time I hadn't thought about the fires in days."

"Or worried about Steve," her best friend replied.

"I'll always worry, but at least the rest of the department is worried, too."

The girls wheeled their bikes into the garage area and hosed off the mud and grime that caked the bicycle chains and tires. Keesha finished first and locked her bike in the rack. As Keesha left for her apartment, Sara stayed with her bike to make sure everything was in tip-top shape. She went into the storage room to get Steve's tool kit. Without the diversion of Keesha's conversation, her mood began to darken. How long would it be until any of them felt really, truly safe?

Her skin began to prickle as images of the charred Jeep blended with the remains of the Patrone deli. An evening with friends was just what she needed.

She grabbed the toolbox and turned to snap off the light. Her stomach tightened. Was someone there? What hadn't she heard? She ached for Tuck's familiar warning signals. She should have gone upstairs with Keesha.

Sara stared at the accumulation of stuff her neighbors kept. There were skis, a set of golf clubs, other toolboxes, and a child's tricycle. She looked at all of it and tried to keep out the rest, the worry and the dread. Then, as she turned around, she got the answer to her gooseflesh. George Burkette was at the other end of the passage.

He looked as startled as she was. She confronted her fear with her most powerful weapon, anger. With her heart racing, she marched down to him. "What are you doing in here? This is private — for residents."

As she spoke, his expression changed. He smiled. "I *am* a resident. I've been moving in all day. I decided to take the studio apartment on the third floor. Number 3C."

I guess that blows what's left of your theory, Bret signed as he and Damon picked up Sara and Keesha a few hours later. *It doesn't make much sense that an arsonist would deliberately move into a building where he knows there's a cop, especially one who has such a personal connection with the case. I'll bet Steve agrees with me*, he added.

Steve doesn't know yet. He doesn't get off his shift until ten. She watched the city streets through the window as Damon drove toward Riverside Drive, then turned back to Bret. *I'd like to be home by then. I want to be there and tell him. I know it's early —*

Be there to tell Steve, or be there to pester him? Sara, you can't be his bodyguard. You know how annoyed you get when he does this to you. At ten o'clock we'll probably be right in the middle of the movie.

My brother's life is in danger! All I'm asking is to get me home early so I can talk to him. If you can't borrow Damon's car, Kim will drive me home or I'll call a cab. I'm sorry I didn't mention it back at the apartment. I could have driven myself . . . unless of course the arsonist had burned up our other car, too.

Bret squeezed his eyebrows together. *Not funny!* he signed.

Sara felt like a stranger at the party. Despite the fact that The Garage was packed with her closest friends, their faces swam in front of her. Even the pizza was tasteless.

At a few minutes after ten Bret tapped his watch and held up Damon's car keys. *I'll take you home. You're not exactly the life of the party.*

Sara circled her heart. *I know. I'm too worried. I'll feel better when I talk to Steve.*

Bret's expression said he knew otherwise.

She wouldn't feel better until the case was solved and Steve was no longer a target.

As Bret pulled the car under the overhang at the entrance to Thurston Court, Sara turned in her seat. *Don't come up with me. I'll be fine.* She leaned over and kissed him as an apology for her behavior.

You sure?

Yes. Liz was about to start the movie and you'll miss it. Go. Really.

Okay. I'll call you tomorrow . . . tell you what you missed.

Sara nodded, hastily opened the door, and waved him off. She could tell he was hurt and angry, but she was too worried to sit in the car and make conversation. She'd have a chance to make it up to him tomorrow.

When she entered the apartment lobby, there wasn't a soul around. A tingling sensation crept up her arms, under her shirt along the back of her neck. She pushed the elevator button. Was it going to be like this forever?

As she got in and hit the button for seven, she shuddered, sure that George Burkette had already discovered which floor, which apartment, which front door was the Howells'.

Sara got off the elevator with her mind racing, half wishing she'd stayed at Liz's. She turned her key in the lock and opened the door. Lights were on, which meant Steve was home. She called his name, anxious to spill everything she knew. It was Tuck who answered by trotting across the foyer from the living room. She knelt to ruffle his fur and stopped with her hand still on his neck as she glanced into the living room. Steve was standing in the middle with two of the officers who'd interviewed her at detective headquarters downtown. They were all looking at George Burkette.

Chapter 24

The shock registered in her face as Steve walked to her. *That's him! I came home to warn you that's he's moved into the building. Are they arresting him? Are you all right?* Her fingers flew as she tried to get information out of Steve.

He frowned as he tried to piece together the portions of ASL he knew. *I'm fine. Say again,* he signed to get her to repeat herself.

She locked her wrists together as if she were being handcuffed, then stepped back in shock as Steve laughed and shook his head.

Instead of replying, he took Sara by the arm and led her to the group and pointed to the coffee table. A small, strange-looking collection of wire with a canister no bigger than a double-A battery was sitting there. Sara looked at her brother.

"George Burkette moved into the building. Tonight he found remnants of this timing device in the garage."

She shook her head. "He found it himself? He came to the police?"

Steve nodded. "You can see it's been flattened and driven on, but George found it up against the wall. He came up here to show me and insisted that I call the arson squad." He had a smug I-told-you-so expression at the corners of his mouth.

Deafness. That would be next. As soon as they were alone Steve would try to explain that because she was deaf she had misunderstood George's intentions, maybe even some of the things he'd said. She leaned over the table to look at the device. Her ears burned. How could she have been so wrong? How could she have misread and misjudged her instincts so badly?

It happened, even to professionals like her father and her brother. Maybe she had been behaving like an amateur. The gut instinct she prided herself on wasn't worth anything unless it was combined with motive and hard evidence. The heat started up from her collar and across her cheeks.

George looked at her, through her, as if he knew everything she'd been thinking since the moment he'd knocked into her in the garage. He knew she'd given his name to the investigators. It was her fault his privacy had been invaded. She apologized by circling her heart. Let him figure out what it meant.

Suddenly he looked away, back at the coffee table. "I wish you could lift some fingerprints from it," he said. "I'm sure not going to feel safe in Thurston Court knowing the arsonist was able to get in here without being noticed."

And what about you getting in here without being noticed? Sara wanted to reply. If you're so innocent, why do I feel like you're guilty?

Sara hadn't slept well in weeks and Saturday night was no exception. She should have felt secure, relaxed with Steve in the apartment, but she lay in bed for what felt like hours and stared at every shadow. After

George Burkette and the officers had left the apartment, Steve had told her that the wires looked to be a perfect match for the remnants scraped from the remains of the Jeep. Being wrong about Burkette was bad enough. It also meant someone else was out there — close — still watching. Still waiting.

The next afternoon Sara unlocked her bike from the rack. She could see Steve kneeling in his parking spot as George pointed to where he had found the wires. Sara pulled her bike into the noon sun and headed for the university district. She was dressed for touring from sunglasses and gloves to helmet and biking shorts, streamlined, as if the wind could peel off her restlessness.

The only thing worse than having to get an I-told-you-so look from a detective was having to take it from a boyfriend. Nevertheless, she needed to tell Bret face-to-face. It wasn't something she wanted to type out on her TTY keyboard. She couldn't stand the thought of sitting and waiting for Bret's terse reply. Instead she called and typed out another biking invitation. He had agreed immediately.

There was nothing left of the night's rain but puddles. Traffic was light. Perfect conditions. She pumped vigorously over the hilly avenues, and kicked up water in the alleys she cut through to avoid the busier boulevards between Thurston Court and Bret's quieter street. She pedaled past the university's veterinary school and turned toward Dr. Agnew's office and Ketchum Fitness Center.

She put her right foot on the curb to keep her balance and coasted slowly so she could see if the gym was busy. In spite of Steve's decision, she hoped enough customers had stuck by Greg that he wouldn't have to close. She shook her head as she looked in the picture window. The lights were off.

On the off chance that Dr. Agnew had Sunday office hours, Sara coasted into the small parking area farther down the block to give her a quick update on Tuck and thank her again for treating the emergency on a Saturday night. Sara wheeled her bike to the door, but the office was closed. Just as well, she thought as she adjusted her glasses. Bret was waiting.

As she walked her bike back to the parking area, a figure darted from around the corner of the building. He was in black from cap to sneakers, and caught the edge of her rear tire. As he careened forward, Sara fell backward with the bike on top of her.

As she came up on one knee she realized who it was and tried to put out her hand. Greg Ketchum shook himself off, however and bolted across the landscaping. Her stomach turned as she caught her breath. He smelled unmistakably of gasoline. The odor lingered as he ran out of sight.

Chapter 25

Alarm sent adrenaline pumping through her as she tried to scramble after him, but by the time she freed herself from her bike and limped around the corner, he was gone. She turned around and ran back to the gym. Black smoke seeped into the air from under the front door and the gym equipment that had been in view in the picture window was obliterated by a curtain of flame.

Others were running, but Sara didn't stay long enough to ask if an alarm was sounding or if the police had been called. She got back on her bike and raced to the Sandersons'. Bret was in the driveway, dressed as she was.

The minute she came into view, he tapped his ears. *Sirens.*

She tossed her sunglasses and bike on the grass and signed frantically in reply. *911. It's the gym. I know who set the fire.*

Before she knew it, Sara was in a squad car, back at the scene. Smoke was now pouring from the fitness center, spewing into the air through the windows smashed by the fire department. It was all too eerily and painfully familiar.

The officer in the front of the car she was riding in picked up his hand-held radio. Another cruiser pulled up to them with its lights flashing. The officer asked her to stay in the backseat, but as she leaned forward, a uniformed patrolman helped Greg Ketchum from the second vehicle and had him stand against the door.

"Is that the guy you saw running from the scene?" the officer asked her.

Sara nodded.

Edward Wilkins tried to make a joke as he arrived in the conference room downtown and patted Sara's shoulder. "A medal from the city won't be enough. We'll have to make you a member of the force."

Sara nodded numbly and wished she could smile. It was worse than a horrible dream. It was a horrible coincidence. "Keep me out of the papers," she said, hoping she was understood. "I don't want any more publicity."

The fire marshall looked apologetic. "We've got the arsonist. You don't have anything to worry about anymore."

"Has he confessed?"

Wilkins looked uncomfortable but nodded his head. "Yes. We found the paint can with the rags, the matches . . . the entire MO fits perfectly. We've already started on the background check. No doubt this guy has connections to a lot more than your brother."

Sara tapped his sleeve. "But he burned his own business."

The fire marshall nodded. "Sure. A perfect cover-up. It was another place associated with your brother and Ketchum made sure it was a total loss. The insurance company would have paid in full."

Sara shivered as she thought of Greg's

bursts of anger she'd witnessed. The deli had burned hours after his fight with Steve at the marina. Steve recommended the rest of the officers at the station also drop their memberships and the Jeep had been destroyed. No doubt the arson squad would find motives for the other fires, as well.

Sara rubbed her eyes and ran her hand through her tangled hair, relieved that Radley's ordeal was finally over.

Bret would be relieved as well. For once it wouldn't bother her to agree she'd jumped to conclusions. It didn't make her like George Burkette any better, but it would feel a lot more comfortable living in the same building with him knowing he wasn't a pyromaniac.

Steve mirrored Sara's emotions. Sunday's relief changed to a deep sadness that permeated everything he did. Even he was silent during the few meals they ate together. Circles formed under his eyes. On the nights he was home, long after Sara had gone to bed, light under her door told her he was fighting insomnia.

At the end of the week when Steve returned home after a visit with Greg at the city jail, Sara decided it was time to get him to talk. "It must be terrible knowing someone you were trying to help came so close to killing you," she said. She circled her heart.

"He could have killed you and Keesha, too. Even tonight he swore he was innocent."

"Steve, I saw him."

Her brother shook his head. "He admits he set the fire at the gym, but he swears he set it up to look like the arsonist had done it so he could collect the insurance money. He swore he knew about the paint can of rags and the matches from the newspaper and TV."

Do you believe him? Is that what's eating at you?

Steve shrugged his shoulders. "I'm a cop. I've seen too many people lie when the whole world trusted them. The investigation is still underway, but they already know he worked part-time for the parks department. I always thought he quit the criminology program at RU, but I found out today he got thrown out for cheating."

Cheating? Let me guess — he copied research papers from the city library. Steve nodded and Sara's heart fell. "But how about the rest, the Blue Onion and the Gates's? You told me Mr. Gates is a banker."

Steve rubbed his eyes. "Robert Gates doesn't know him, but he's president of the bank that turned down Greg's application for a loan to keep the gym going. The mayor, city council . . . they're all pressuring Ed Wilkins to close the case."

What do you think?

Steve paced across the kitchen as anger deepened his complexion. If he were shouting, she figured he had good reason. "I don't know. I don't want to believe it. I'm too close to it to be objective."

She tapped her temple and raised her eyebrows.

"Objective," Steve repeated. "I can't tell. It's a damn good thing it's not for me to decide."

"Maybe you're right." *Right. Maybe he's telling the truth.*

Truth? Steve repeated.

Sara nodded. "If he's crazy enough to try to burn houses, then why didn't he burn the house of the loan officer who turned him down? How would he know Gates was the bank president? Why not burn a college building instead of the library research room? The university kicked him out, not the city library."

Steve looked at her with pain in his eyes. *What?* she signed. *What else?*

He came back to the table and sat down slowly. "The fitness center wasn't a total loss. This afternoon in Greg's desk they found pieces of the same kind of wire that was used to start the Jeep fire."

Chapter 26

Puffy white clouds dusted the sky as Sara glanced at the assembled police officers, fire-fighters, and city officials. How ironic, she thought. The last time these people gathered for a Howell it was for my father's funeral. She wondered if her parents would be proud of this moment or as uncomfortable as she was.

The mayor introduced the fire marshall and as Edward Wilkins stepped forward, Suzanne Andrews got ready to interpret. The city council had wanted everything perfect for the presentation of Sara's humanitarian award, right down to someone to translate the speeches into ASL. As far as Sara knew, there weren't any other deaf people in attendance, but it was a nice gesture. Politically correct. The mayor was up for reelection.

She scanned the crowd. Lots of friends and familiar faces with smiles and we're-so-proud-of-you expressions. She waved at Charlie Gates. The entire Patrone family was there, next to the Fletchers. In the back, off to the side, she spotted George Burkette. For once she wasn't surprised to see him. He'd come by the apartment again, this time with a bottle of wine for Steve in honor of Greg Ketchum's arrest. Now he looked as intense as ever.

The mayor stepped to the podium and jabbered about being tough on crime. He announced what the media had been using as the lead story for a week: The arsonist was safely behind bars. Sara doubted that there was anyone within twenty miles who didn't know the name Gregory Ketchum or the fate of his fitness center. At least it had kept her out of the headlines for a while. Until today.

Steve nudged her and she turned to pay attention to Mrs. Andrews's interpreting. . . . *Sara Howell, an example for all of us, an outstanding member of the Radley community whose family has already gone beyond the call of duty for citizens like us . . .*

I'm no hero, she wanted to sign back. She scanned the crowd, not for familiar faces, but for the unfamiliar. It was getting harder and harder to trust anyone.

Chapter 27

Enough about her! He lay on his back with his fingers pressed against the pain in his temples and looked at the four walls. His scrapbook would have made him feel better, but he'd had to hide it. Couldn't keep it in here. He winced. The snake was coiled again, ready to strike. It would be tougher now, of course, but he'd find a way. He always found a way.

Chapter 28

Steve replaced his Jeep with a similar model in an identical shade of blue. After the ceremony, as he drove to the Side Door Café, Sara sat next to Bret in the backseat and wished it could be so easy for all the victims to replace what they'd lost.

"There's a good chance that Greg Ketchum will be released on bail until his trial," Steve said to Marisa as they waited for their meals to arrive.

The popular spot was crowded again. The college semester was nearly over and since Greg Ketchum's arrest the city hadn't had more than accidental kitchen fires and a blaze in a faulty air conditioner.

Will they let him out with all those charges against him? Bret signed.

Steve shrugged. *"Don't know.* It wouldn't be the first time a high-powered lawyer pulled the rug out from under the police department."

Marisa sat up in alarm. "Not without a psychiatrist's report! How could a judge think Greg is sane enough —"

Steve tried to look reassuring. "Thanks for the concern. A judge could easily agree with Ketchum's attorney. Greg has no prior record, not even a parking ticket. So far there's nothing linking him to the other fires except circumstantial evidence."

"Circumstantial, but the same kind of wires were in his desk. The Jeep fire could have been murder," Sara added.

Steve looked at each of them. "As a detective, I have to admit that it could also be unrelated to the arsonist."

"And related to some other case you're involved in?" Marisa asked.

Steve sighed before he answered and then nodded. "I don't mean that it wasn't deliberate, but the timing device hasn't shown up at any of the other fires. No other cars have been burned. It's not the first time I've had threats against me, for that matter."

Sara watched her brother try to be honest and not frighten Marisa at the same time. The way Dad always treated us, she thought with a sudden ache. No panic; no hysterics; but no glossing over the truth; no lies to keep us in the dark, either. Not till the last time. She held her breath until the tears passed. Chills ran up her back and she turned in her seat as if Greg Ketchum might have already walked through the entrance.

To force herself into a better mood, Sara turned to Bret and brought up a far more pleasant subject. Keesha's seventeenth birthday was a week away and they were giving her a This Is Your Life surprise party.

The Blue Onion was about to reopen and Keesha swore she was dying to go back. It was all Damon had needed to ask her to dinner. Bret had decided it would be the perfect cover while the rest of Keesha's friends gathered at The Garage. It would be natural for Damon and Keesha to stop by the Martinsons' after dinner to see what everybody else was doing.

To hide the cars, Kim Roth volunteered her street at Winchester Commons, farther down Riverside Drive. Liz had already asked that the group go through their old scrapbooks and albums for any funny childhood photographs that might include Keesha. After the weeks of terror and chaos, they were all anxious for some laughs.

When Sara mentioned it at school to Brenda Fletcher, Brenda offered to pack a box of mementos and leave it in the Thurston Court storage room the afternoon of the party.

Now, as Sara and Bret discussed it, he added that the owner of the Blue Onion would probably be thrilled to have some kids back to help get business back to normal.

Back to normal, Sara repeated. *It's about time.*

As usual, Sara, Keesha, and Liz spent Saturday morning together at the boathouse with the rest of the crew team. The stretch of bad weather had cleared and warm, clear weather had been forecast for the weekend. It made the workout on the water fun and anticipation for the night all the better.

When she got back to Thurston Court, Steve was getting ready for work. Sara showered, changed, and crossed the hall for lunch at the Fletchers'. Brenda Fletcher served them chicken salad and winked as she put down the plates. Done, Sara thought, wondering how much Keesha's mother was able to stuff into a box.

Forty minutes later as Sara left for her apartment, her own front door opened. George Burkette waved as he continued down the hall and pushed the button for the elevator. She could have sworn he said, "Have fun tonight."

What was that all about? she demanded of Steve the minute she was inside.

Her brother shrugged. "He gave me two tickets to the ten o'clock performance tonight at Maxwell's, the comedy club on Carson Street."

"Great. Now he wants to be your best friend?"

Steve shook his head. "I doubt it. He just

said he can't use them and he doesn't know anybody else who lives in our building. I told him you had plans, but Marisa and I both get off work at ten so I took them."

Why can't he use them?

"To be honest, I didn't ask. I don't like the guy much. I don't want to get a friendship going. I wouldn't even have taken the tickets except he said he was going to throw them out."

I'm glad you did. I'll know where you are, Sara signed.

"I suppose you'd feel better if Lieutenant Marino came along?"

You've given me a police escort in the past. Great idea for you, too. Can never be too careful, right?

As planned, that evening Marcus called Sara on her TTY to signal that Damon and Keesha were about to leave the Fletchers'.

"Blue Onion?" Sara signed innocently as she pretended to run into them as they waited for the elevator.

"Keesha's choice," Damon replied.

Sara suggested they swing by Liz's after

dinner. The minute the elevator closed on the couple, Sara ran back to her apartment. It was nearly eight. Bret and the rest of the group would already be at Liz's setting out the memorabilia and hanging the posters Kim had made from some of the photos.

Sara took time to style her hair with a new clip and add some makeup, then locked up and rode the elevator to the lobby. Her last errand was to remind John O'Connor, the doorman, to give Tuck a quick walk around ten. As the elevator opened, she glanced across the lobby at the glass-enclosed entrance. Greg Ketchum was standing at the intercom, pressing the buzzer marked HOWELL.

Chapter 29

Before Sara had time to think, Greg slammed one fist into the other and pushed his way out through the entrance doors.

Even after talking to John O'Connor, who hadn't spoken to him and didn't recognize him, Sara's pulse refused to slow down. The words "out on bail" pounded in her head as she shoved open the fire door and hurried down the flight of stairs to the basement. She tried not to think about it as she unlocked the storage room. She was late enough. Other things were important. As if seeing the accused arsonist at her door hadn't rattled her enough, she opened the storage room and found three sealed cardboard boxes. Each looked like it could be the one from Brenda

Fletcher. One was tied with twine, one with masking tape, and one with duct tape. None of them had a name on it.

Sara had nothing to open them with, so she grabbed all three, slung her bag over her shoulder and carried them into the garage.

Steve's parking spot was empty. He'd driven to the station. She wished she had time to stop there on her way and tell him who she'd seen — and where.

Sara reached Riverside Drive as the setting sun skimmed the trees. The imposing house had a sweeping back lawn that stopped at the bluff above the river. The wooden garage was set behind the house.

As planned the entire area was clear of cars. As Sara pulled up to the garage, Liz drove in behind her. "So far everything's perfect," Liz said, then slid a cake from the backseat. "My folks won't be back till eleven. When Damon gets Keesha here, she'll think it's just you and Bret hanging out with me. Wait till you see how much stuff we've got. Kim wanted to hang balloons out here on the railing, but that would have given everything away."

As they climbed the steps to the converted apartment, Liz nodded at the intricate wooden bannister that ran up the stairs to a balcony and the second-floor entrance, but Sara was barely paying attention.

Three boxes? Bret signed as he put them on the floor.

Sara shrugged. She began to sign. *I need you to call Steve.*

Liz has a TTY in the house, Bret replied.

No time. Call and tell him K-E-T-C-H-U-M is out on bail.

Bret reacted nearly as strongly as she had. Anger tightened his mouth the moment she signed that he'd been to the apartment. He grabbed her wrist and they made their way to the phone in the little kitchen.

Sara stared at Bret as he spoke, trying to decipher every word. The conversation, however, was brief. Steve was out on assignment. Lieutenant Marino took the message and replied that Steve had already been informed and had planned to tell Sara himself.

She says not to worry. He's under surveillance. Everything will be fine.

Fine! Sara replied.

Bret hugged her. *Steve's with his partner and you know exactly where he'll be at ten. Sara, they wouldn't have agreed to bail if they thought he was dangerous.*

Sara turned around as Liz tapped her on the shoulder, anxious to get the boxes open. Sara started slicing the twine from the largest box. It was full of Christmas tree ornaments and old cards addressed to the Webster family on the fifth floor. "I don't think that's from Keesha's mom," Bret said, before sliding it under the end table.

Even as Sara sliced the masking tape from the second one, her mind was elsewhere. Greg Ketchum could be anywhere. Sara hastily pulled the box flaps open. Brenda Fletcher had packed an eight-by-ten of her daughter grinning with no front teeth, a teddy bear, even a few photographs of Sara and Keesha as seven-year-olds. At the bottom of the box was a collection of early school papers.

* * *

By the time Damon and Keesha arrived and she got over her shock, it was nearly ten. As Sara watched her best friend open her gifts, she told herself that soon Steve would be safely seated at the comedy club with his arm around Marisa. Soon they'd sit and laugh themselves silly.

Keesha finished opening her gag gifts and explaining the memorabilia. *"Only a mother who's a principal would think to pack school papers as a surprise!"* She passed around her sixth-grade essay on whales while Liz cut the cake.

Bret laughed and handed the essay to Kim, then turned to Sara. *We never opened the other box. Any chance Keesha's mom packed two? Maybe Marcus sent something.*

Sara pulled it out from under the end table. *I never thought of that.* She sliced through the tape and opened the flaps. A scrapbook was on top of what appeared to be folders. *Maybe you're right.* She held the scrapbook up and tried to get Keesha's attention, but Kim had taken her across the room. Rather than wait, Sara opened the cover.

Color photographs filled the first pages,

but there were no African-American faces. Sara was about to close the scrapbook when she looked closer. In two of the photographs a boy with tousled blond hair stood in front of a typical Radley house. In the third he was in the backyard in a soccer uniform. Sara frowned.

No Fletchers? Bret signed.

Alarm, not deafness, kept her silent. She tapped the photographs. *Look at the house! This is fire house. This is the one!*

Bret straightened up and stared at her. *How do you know? Sara, you're jumping to conclusions —*

She squinted with her heart pounding against her ribs and jabbed her finger on the first one. Her nail blotted out the person, but pointed to the tiny numbers over the front porch: 5437.

Five, four, three, seven. Before she'd finished signing, Bret turned and worked his way through the crowd to the kitchen. He came back with the Radley phone book and slid his finger down the G column until it rested on GATES, Robt & Mrgt 5437 Reynolds.

"Oh my God." Sara tried to keep down her anxiety.

Bret pressed his fingers on Sara's lips to tell her not to speak. He was right. There was no sense in involving anybody else.

Sara looked into Bret's worried expression. *This must be George Burkette's scrapbook. He had it hidden in the storage room in case the police searched his apartment. This is why the police couldn't find a connection from Burkette to Gates. There isn't one. The connection is the house.* She stabbed at the child in the photo. *This is George Burkette. He burned his childhood house.*

Chapter 30

Bret turned the page. There were school pictures and family shots. On the third page there was a newspaper clipping. An older version of the same child was cutting a ribbon in front of what appeared to be new landscaping.

DEXTER FAMILY DONATES LAND FOR SANCTUARY IN CITY PARK. GEORGE BURKETTE, STEPSON OF HENRY DEXTER, CUTS THE RIBBON TO DEDICATE . . .

Sara didn't read another line. Instead she flipped the pages. HENRY DEXTER DONATES HISTORIC DOCUMENTS TO RPL headed a half-page column from a Radley Public Library newsletter.

He burned his stepfather's park. I'll bet his stepfather's collection at the library was in that room that burned. He burned the house. Everything has a connection to his stepfather.

Until you got all the attention, Bret replied. *That's when the letter to the Gazette was written. Sara, when nothing changed he must have turned all that rage on your brother for not keeping you out of the spotlight.*

She slammed the book as Bret looked back in the box. His brown eyes darkened as he handed her a wad of electrical wire. It was a match to the wire fragments George Burkette had insisted that he'd found near Steve's parking place. All of it matched the timing device that had ignited the Jeep.

As Sara jumped from the couch, Bret caught her arm.

She shook him off. *There's no time to go through the rest. He gave Steve and Marisa tickets to the comedy club tonight. It's George Burkette. Greg was telling the truth about burning his own gym. I was right all along.*

George even called the police and pretended to find evidence at Steve's parking space. He's crazy, Bret. He's set Steve up and he's going to torch the club!

For once, I believe you. I just don't want to panic anybody.

Sara nodded. *Nobody here is in danger. Just in case, you stay here and keep an eye out for anything — anything at all. Use your ears. I'll drive to the club and get Steve out.* She crossed her heart. *I promise, nothing dangerous. I'll just get him, show him the scrapbook and get him to go back to the police station. From there he can make everything official.*

Liz interrupted them with another offer of cake. "What gives, you two? You're over here signing a mile a minute —"

"Bret will explain," Sara replied. "Liz, your car is blocking mine, can I use it for a quick errand? I have to go talk to Steve. I won't be long."

"Use my TTY in my bedroom. My parents won't be home for another hour, but the key —"

Sara shook her head. "I need to do this in person."

Liz nodded and pulled her car keys from her pocket.

Sara forced herself to obey the speed limit as she left Riverside Drive and headed across town to Carson Street. It was just after ten. The comedy show was about to begin. She gripped the wheel. The wire. Not only had Burkette planted it near Steve's parking space, he must have planted it in Greg Ketchum's desk after the fire at the fitness center. She rapped her fingers impatiently on the steering wheel as she waited for a red light to change, then reached over and touched the scrapbook. She was nauseous with fear for Steve. Evidence, she thought to settle her nerves. At least I have evidence.

Sara double-parked in front of Maxwell's. With the scrapbook and wire in hand, she raced to the ticket window half expecting to see flames. "Manager," she said as clearly as possible. "I'm deaf. Emergency inside." Steve and Marisa were paged and in the lobby in two minutes.

Understand? she signed over and over as Steve and Marisa strained to follow her speech.

Yes! Yes, of course. Steve pulled her into the lighted foyer and opened the evidence. She showed him the first two pages. He looked her straight in the eye. "Go back to Liz's and get the whole box. Meet me at the precinct station. Don't come anywhere near here. Don't go to the apartment. Get the box and come to the Penn Street station."

Of course. I can be back in twenty minutes.

Steve pulled out his police badge. "I have to get to a phone. We need to evacuate this building as calmly as possible and get a dragnet started. You just go get all the evidence and meet me at the station." *Understand? Don't panic anyone at the party.*

Sara hugged them both. *Be careful.*

They both nodded.

* * *

Sara drove Liz's car back, calming herself with the knowledge that Marisa and her brother were in control. By the time she reached Riverside Drive, the evacuation would have begun.

They'll find you, she said to herself. They'll find you and you won't hurt anybody again. She gritted her teeth against the unwanted tears as she thought of Emilio Patrone and Charlie Gates.

She parked Liz's car on the street so she could get her own car out of the driveway, and took another look at the scrapbook. Anger and curiosity kept her turning the pages. These were pages of rage, not happy memories. Somewhere a team of professionals would unlock George Burkette's hatred of his stepfather.

Toward the back of the book, the childhood collection changed to neatly clipped articles of each fire. Two of the earliest were a year old. Sara had still been at Edgewood. All the *Gazette*'s coverage was there: the Library, the Blue Onion, Dexter Sanctuary.

Each was meticulously laid out with notation on the date, time of day. The final section, however, was different. The article on Reynolds Street was torn, almost mutilated, then fit back together and glued on the paper.

The article on her from the Young Living section was a mass of smoothed-out wrinkles, as if it had been balled up and thrown away first. The last entry was a double spread. On the left was the article from the award ceremony. DEAF TEEN AWARDED RADLEY'S HUMANITARIAN MEDAL was filled with tiny burn marks. Cigarette-sized brown-edged holes filled the paper. On the facing page were snapshots taken with an instant camera. Sara looked at images of herself going into the deli, unpacking the Jeep, rowing on the Buckeye. She suddenly understood.

Me. She looked out through the windshield. It wasn't Steve after all.

Fear coursed through her shoulder blades. She looked at the Martinsons' rambling, welcoming house. Me. Tonight. George had given Steve the tickets to get him out of the way for the evening. And if he's here, all he's seen is my car in the driveway. He thinks I'm in there with Liz. He doesn't know the place is crowded with —

She couldn't finish the thought. Instead Sara shoved the scrapbook on the floor of Liz's car and raced across the front lawn. As she headed down the long driveway she could see the lights behind drawn curtains in the second-story windows over the garage doors. Why did Keesha's party have to be a surprise? A normal party would be in the yard, around the pool. Her friends would be safely out here or on the balcony looking at the river. Instead they were all crammed inside the garage, perfect for another tragedy, bigger than George Burkette had ever imagined.

She ran down the gravel. Had he already packed the garage with gasoline-soaked rags? He was cleverer now. He had timers, incendiary devices that ignited by wires. She stopped. She had no idea how they worked, but George Burkette didn't even need to be here to burn Liz Martinson's garage to cinders.

He was here. She could feel it. There's no way he would miss this one. He's here, watching me. He knows I'm back.

Chapter 31

Sara forced herself to walk. The curving gravel driveway seemed to go on forever. The back of her neck tingled. He's crazy. He's determined. Chills tightened her skin into gooseflesh, but she didn't turn around. She shoved her hand in her pocket and curled her fingers over the wire, then walked as calmly as she could toward the wooden staircase that ran along the side of the garage. Every friend she'd made in Radley was in the rooms at the top.

Her mind raced far faster than her body. You're out there, her mind screamed, but you're not going to win. Then she saw the rags stuffed on the stair risers and smelled the gasoline. The paint can was on its side in the grass.

George Burkette was standing in the shrubbery. He was dressed as always in his cap and black sweatshirt. "You've ruined everything," he said as he came into the floodlight. "Do you know how long it took to get him to pay attention to me?"

"Your stepfather?"

He didn't give any indication that he'd understood. "Now he finally understands. He understands all of it. I got rid of his gardens. I ruined his house."

Sara caught a fraction of what he was saying. "The Blue Onion?"

"One more building he owns, one more way to show him." Suddenly Bret and Liz appeared on the balcony and George yanked her away from the garage. It gave her a better view of her friends.

She signed, *Call 911. Fire. Police. Get them here. He's after me, not Steve. Don't come down the stairs. Get out the back windows. Gasoline! It's set to go.*

"Enough!" George yelled as he shook her.

"I was getting even. People were paying attention until you took it all away. Deaf.

Hero. I have to show you, too. All of you need to pay attention."

He looked eerily calm and she thought he might sit down from exhaustion, but instead he grabbed her in a vicelike grip. With his free hand he pulled something from his pocket. As she tried to wrestle free, he snapped his wrist.

Her car exploded. The garage doors blew in as flames shot up the wall. Fire snaked up the stairs, racing from rag to rag until the wall of flame blocked the exit. Thick choking smoke curled from the front. Sara was sure everyone was screaming. She prayed Bret had already called in the emergency.

The heat was unbearable as the flames formed an arc of fire at the stairs. By the time George forced her to run, the sickeningly familiar sight of flashing police and fire equipment lit the sky.

As he dragged her deeper into the shadows at the back of the lawn, Sara could see her friends jumping or working their way down bedsheets. She could see Bret, Damon, Kim helping others and picking up what had been thrown from the kitchen and bedroom windows. Even across the Martinsons' rolling lawn, she could feel the heat of the flames. Smoke burned her throat. It smelled hot and damp. Soot covered her and she realized the fire department had already begun to douse the fire.

George was screaming for them to stop. His hold was so tight she could feel his chest expand as he yelled. His muscles clenched as he continued to drag her back. It was dark; they were well beyond the floodlights. The smoke obliterated the moon.

She knew the lawn well. Frisbee, croquet, volleyball . . . whatever Liz organized was set up close to the house to avoid the ravine that fell hundreds of feet below to the river. As if he suddenly sensed her fear, George turned around and began to push her forward. Smoke stung her throat.

George began to cough and let go to wipe his sleeve. As he swung his arm, Sara lunged and hit him in the middle of the back. He grabbed her but he'd reached the bluff and lost his balance. The two of them slid down the steep embankment, through the underbrush. Branches and twigs sliced and tore as she skittered feetfirst into the ravine. As she caught herself in a jumble of vines, Burkette crashed like dead weight through a branch and down the hill until she lost him in the dark.

She lay tangled in the vines as flashlight beams reached her. They bounced off her legs and illuminated the undergrowth and the broken, gutted path where Burkette had slid past her. In another minute she was tangled in arms, hands, and hugs as Bret slid down next to her and immediately called to the others.

They crawled and inched their way back up to a yard filling with paramedics, firefighters, police, and the remains of Keesha's party.

Patrick and Gloria Martinson had arrived and were helping their daughter turn on the lights on the back porch; the partygoers had moved, or were being helped, into the safety of the pool area. Marisa was even there, ministering to the scrapes, cuts, and more serious injuries from the hasty escapes.

Steve came barreling out of the smoky mist and grabbed Sara. "I was evacuating

Maxwell's when Bret called in the emergency," he said. *Bret called the station and they got me on C-A-R-S-O-N Street.*

Sara pointed to the ravine and Steve nodded. "Burkette's alive. He's down there screaming that this is all his stepfather's fault."

EMT's lifted a semiconscious George Burkette into the ambulance while Steve finished talking with Ed Wilkins. Sara huddled with the rest of the party on the Martinsons' porch and tried to apologize before her own trip to the hospital for a thorough going-over.

"Never apologize for being a hero. You saved us all tonight." Keesha replied. *Hero.*

"I'm no hero! I want a nice normal life." She looked at her brother as he climbed the steps. "Have the police tried to contact Henry Dexter yet?"

Steve shook his head as Marisa tried to brush dirt from his hair and soot from his cheek. "Henry Dexter, Burkette's stepfather, died some time last year. Ed Wilkins just told me he thinks he can trace the first small fires all the way back to the week of the funeral."

"George didn't have the guts to express how angry he was until his stepfather was dead." Sara shivered and leaned into Bret's hug.

Detective or psychiatrist, Bret signed as he kissed her. *There's no doubt you're going to wind up as one or the other.*

Sara kissed him back. *Before I get to that stage of my life, I want time like everybody else to enjoy this one.*

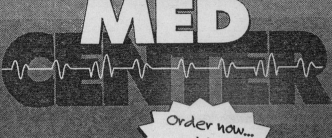